Death Comes to Jane Austen Town

Rosemary Stevens

Contents

Dedication   1

1. Chapter One   2

2. Chapter Two   15

3. Chapter Three   28

4. Chapter Four   37

5. Chapter Five   50

6. Chapter Six   59

7. Chapter Seven   71

8. Chapter Eight   79

9. Chapter Nine   94

10. Chapter Ten   107

11. Chapter Eleven   116

12. Chapter Twelve   129

13. Chapter Thirteen   136

14. Chapter Fourteen   149

15. Chapter Fifteen   157

16. Chapter Sixteen   168

17. Chapter Seventeen   180

18. Chapter Eighteen   189

19. Chapter Nineteen   200

20. Chapter Twenty   208

21. Chapter Twenty-One   218

22. Chapter Twenty-Two   227

23. Epilogue   244

24. RECIPES   254

25. Special Thanks   262

Also by Rosemary Stevens   264

This book is dedicated with love to my son, Tom.

Chapter One

My phone chimed with a new text, jolting me from my dreams. "Have you no compassion for my poor nerves?" I mumbled, rolling over in bed.

I pressed my fingertips to my still closed lids. Maybe the simple action would hold back the reality of last Friday. Maybe I could return to blessed sleep and dream of well-mannered ladies and gentlemen performing English country dances while discreetly flirting. A place where no rude regional managers dropped by unannounced in their BMWs and designer sunglasses with disastrous news for my hometown.

Maybe not.

With a sigh, I opened my eyes and sat up.

My heart sank as Friday's horror played out in my mind. The moment where I, Kay Starling, made a substantial portion of my hometown, Boring, Virginia, jobless. Unemployed. Laid-off.

Including myself.

"Effective immediately, The Boring, Virginia Hurdee Gurdee bottling plant will close permanently. As you leave, you will be given envelopes that include two weeks' severance pay and a coupon worth

a dollar off your next Hurdee Gurdee purchase. Thank you for your attention." My voice had shaken as I read the announcement. Mr. Harvey, Hurdee Gurdee Regional Manager and World Champion Coward, had made me, as head of the Human Relations Department, drop the prepared bombshell.

I'd spent the weekend trying to distract myself, hiding in my four-poster bed and watching—twice, mind you—the 1995 six-part, three hundred-and-twenty-seven-minute-long BBC television adaptation of Jane Austen's *Pride and Prejudice*. What else could a Janeite be expected to do in times of extreme stress?

In between reciting lines out loud along with the characters onscreen, I shouted advice and comments as well.

Immersing myself in Jane Austen's story was the medicine I needed to help me forget Friday, if even for a little while, and I gave myself a whopping dose.

Thinking now of Colin Firth as Mr. Darcy made me turn my head to see his likeness hanging above my bookshelf which, appropriately, boasted multiple editions of each of Austen's six novels.

Dragging myself out of bed, I took a moment to gaze at Darcy. Not for me a staid portrait of the gentleman in coat and cravat, although that one hung downstairs. This photo was full-on Darcy emerging from the lake at Pemberley, Regency shirt plastered to his chest. True, the scene from the adaptation was not in the book, but one must make allowances for, um, creativity.

I picked up my phone to read the text.

Kay! Family breakfast meeting in 30 minutes. Do not be late! A

So, Aunt Adeline had called a rare Monday breakfast meeting. Sunday family dinners at Starling Farm? A weekly occurrence. Breakfast? Not so much. Aunt Adeline was up to something.

Grabbing fresh clothes, I ambled toward the bathroom.

Ten minutes later, refreshed by my shower, I towel dried my brunette bob, drew in a deep breath, and pulled myself together. No more wallowing in self-pity. Nothing that had happened on Friday was my fault, although it felt that way. Mr. Harvey had made me the messenger of doom, that's all.

Still, I grimaced as flashes flitted through my mind's eye of the employees' shocked faces when I had gathered everyone together and told them that what had been the Hurdee Gurdee soda bottling plant for almost fifty years was no more. No more chocolate flavored sweet tea soda would be bottled in Boring. And the coupon? What an insult. As if anyone in Boring would be caught dead drinking the soda again.

I remembered Eric Longo, packaging worker and father of three, stunned. He and his wife, Lorraine, had bought their first house three months ago in June. Lorraine was expecting their fourth child after Christmas.

Darla Bicknell, line worker and mother of the cutest four-year old, Barrett Leigh, burst into tears at the news.

My own sister, Josie, head of admin, her mouth in a grim line.

Josie's administrative assistant, Sharon, whose son Palmer was in his first year at VCU Medicine determined to be a doctor, had a blank look of shock on her face.

My neighbors. My friends. Members of the community I loved. Now unemployed in a town of 1455 people where there weren't a lot of ways to earn a living. How would they feed their families?

I threw my towel into a circular cloth laundry basket depicting the spines of Jane Austen's novels. After raking a comb through my hair, I applied a tiny amount of styling gel to tame my waves. Sunscreen, a couple of passes with the mascara wand, and some tinted lip balm completed my beauty routine.

Clad in my summer uniform, a short-sleeved, cotton, floral, midi dress and white tennis shoes, I tidied the room, made my bed, and started downstairs. On the landing half-way down, I paused and ran my hand along the blue damask wallpaper. Out of the window and across the perfectly cut green grass of Starling Farm, I could see The Secrets Tree, a creeping cherry tree about two dozen feet wide with branches hanging down to the ground. Under it, my best friend Hayley and I had shared confidences since grade school.

Further back was the grass riding ring, the stables, a low clapboard building that served as an office, and in the distance, across gently rolling terrain and wrapped in a late summer blue haze, the Blue Ridge Mountains.

Starling Farm consisted of a seven-bedroom red brick house, built in 1778 in the Federal Style, that had been my home since birth and sat on ninety-five acres of land. My brother, Hugo, lived in a ginormous converted apartment over one of the stables that wasn't in use. A brick ranch house on the grounds accommodated my sister, Josie, and her family. Only my other brother, Neil, lived in Boring proper.

As I stood dawdling at the window, bright September sunshine warmed my face and made me frown. How could it be bright and cheerful outside? Shouldn't it be gloomy with a storm overhead like a scene from the gothic *Northanger Abbey*?

The faint sound of a horse whinnying made me glance toward the newer stables. Hugo's tall figure made his way toward the house. He had the looks in our family, reminding people of a young Warren Beatty. His English springer spaniel mix, Bowie, stayed close to Hugo's jean-clad legs and walked with a jaunty step, his excitement to have Hugo home evident.

Over by the brick folly surrounded by maple trees, I saw the usual crowd of squirrels, birds, chipmunks, and crows had gathered for their breakfast. I ran down the rest of the stairs and dashed out the back door onto the flagstone terrace. "Wait for me! I'll be right there!" I called to Hugo.

Receiving a nod and a careless wave in response to my plea, I went over to the folly, my private sanctuary. I retrieved bags of wild bird food and peanuts from inside. With no time to linger, I made quick work of filling feeders and bowls.

I paused with the bag in hand while topping off a bowl of peanuts. A shiny orange Hurdee Gurdee bottle cap had been placed on the ground next to the bowl.

"Caw! Caw!" called one of my regular crows who occasionally left me a present.

"That's not funny, Henry Tilney! Badly done indeed!" I scolded.

He was still cawing in crow-laughter as I hurried back toward the house and caught up with Hugo.

"Hey, sis," my brother said, his expression somber. "You weren't talking to the squirrels and birds again, were you?"

"Don't be silly." I petted the now dancing brown and white dog and then threw myself into my brother's hug. "You're here. I thought you might still be up in Middleburg."

He held the door open for me and we entered the house via the mudroom, Bowie at his heels. "I finished my business in horse country. Picked up a stallion. Great pedigree and an even temperament."

I turned toward him, my voice low. "Listen, I know you want to recreate the success Uncle Curtis had breeding horses, but you're too hard on yourself."

Hugo gazed out the small window in the direction of the stables. "Curtis was smart. Back in the day, the Starling name meant something in horse breeding circles because Curtis Starling was in charge."

"Uncle Curtis died five years ago. He was seventy-eight and had spent his life building up the business. You're only twenty-nine. Give yourself a chance."

He gave me a rueful half-smile. "No one in our family has had the talent for success since Uncle Curtis. Mom and Dad never cared about the horses, just their archeology. Always away on digs. Where are they now?"

"Peru. Come on, they've been wonderful parents to us. You can't blame them for having a passion outside of horses."

Hugo shrugged and said, "By the way, when I left Middleburg, I left Mitzi drinking champagne with the bloodstock agent who sold me the stallion."

Ugh. Mitzi with her hair extensions and lip injections always looking for a rich man to fund her Instagram life. That was only my opinion, though. She was, or had been, Hugo's latest girlfriend. "Are you okay?"

"Yeah, it wasn't that serious." He bent and scratched behind the dog's ears. Then he straightened and smiled, "I hear you've been burning down the town."

I punched him playfully in the arm and opened the kitchen door. "Please don't tease. It's a sore subject."

"The town will forgive you."

"You think so?"

"In about ten years," he assured me.

"As if I'm not feeling bad enough." I side-eyed him and then gave my attention to the country-styled kitchen. The long farm-house table was covered in a classic red checkered tablecloth and laden with dishes. Aunt Adeline had likely been cooking since before the sun came up.

Nestled in blue willow china were scrambled eggs, Virginia ham, buttermilk biscuits and gravy, cheesy grits, bacon, pancakes, and toast. There was a carafe of orange juice and a pot of tea alongside jars of orange marmalade and cherry preserves and a glass container of maple syrup.

"Good morning, Hugo, you scamp. There's a fresh pot of coffee on the counter. I'll forgive you two for being the last to arrive," said Aunt Adeline from her place at the head of the table.

Almost sixty-five and a lifelong Janeite, Aunt Adeline was dressed in a Regency style, striped cherry red and white muslin gown. Her dark hair, heavily peppered with gray, was topped with a red scarf artfully tied into a Regency headband. She met my gaze. "Kay, it's not your fault the bottling plant closed. You need to stop thinking that way *tout de suite.*"

"Yes, ma'am," I replied. Aunt Adeline has always had a way of reading my mind. She's also one of the most competent women I know and a beloved member of the community. The fact that she wears Regency clothes is a way to express herself, to show her love of Jane Austen. That love had been passed down through my family for generations going back to our ancestors, who were from England and were some of the founders of Boring. My fingers went to the gold silhouette charm of Austen that hung on a gold chain around my neck. Aunt Adeline wore an identical one.

"Kay! Sit next to me and tell us what happened last Friday. Don't leave anything out," my brother Neil commanded, stuffing a biscuit dripping in honey into his mouth with one hand and pulling out a chair for me with the other.

Where Hugo's hair was dark like mine, Neil's hair ventured into the dark blond category. At thirty-one he was two years older than Hugo and four years older than me. The owner and publisher of the town newspaper, *The Boring Bugle*, and the most curious person I knew, his greeting wasn't surprising.

"Good morning to you, too, Neil," I said with a smile and sat down.

My eldest sibling, Josephine, who everyone calls Josie, handed her husband, Bobby Rice, the plate of bacon. "I was there," she said. "That wimp Mr. Harvey, made Kay make the announcement. I heard the plant manager, Mr. Samuels, had already taken off in his truck for parts unknown."

"Ruined!" Bobby declared between bites of bacon. "The whole town is ruined now that the plant is closed. How are people supposed to buy groceries?"

Bobby was the manager and part-owner of Starling's Grocery. He resembled a cuddly teddy bear with his short curly blond hair and his ever-growing tummy.

"I have an idea about that," Aunt Adeline said. She was the majority owner of Starling's Grocery. "Been cogitating on it. Not quite ready yet, but getting there."

"When businesses go, so do jobs," Hugo said. He slid a piece of bacon to Bowie who lay across his feet under the table. "Plus, you know how it is here in Boring. You have to set your mental clock back fifty years."

I accepted the plate of eggs, ham, and biscuits Aunt Adeline passed me. "That's not a bad thing. So we're an old-fashioned community in some ways. Nothing wrong with that."

"You would say that, Kay," Hugo said. "Half the time you live in Regency England."

"I do not!" I shot back. *A quarter of the time at most, your lordship.*

Aunt Adeline glanced at him and cleared her throat.

Hugo mumbled a "Sorry" and turned his attention to his food.

I looked at my sister. "What are you going to do, Josie?"

She paused before answering me. One hand reached up to fiddle with the gold, heart stud earrings she always wore. Bobby had given them to her when they graduated high school. "Bobby and I talked about it. You know me, I like a project. I'm going to renovate the cabins out at Starling Lake. I'm fairly skilled with carpentry, and I can work on making curtains on weekends with Sarah Beth's help, if I can pry her away from her books. I know it's a lot of work, but I'm up for it."

Josie's daughter, Sarah Beth, started seventh grade this morning. Although Josie wasn't really a Janeite, she read Austen. Sarah Beth was a precocious, strong reader and definitely a Janeite Junior. I may have had a hand in that. I nodded at Josie now. "You'll do a great job and renting the cabins out again will be another income source for you."

"If I can entice people out there," Josie said. "I have to figure out an angle for that."

"What about you, Kay?" Neil asked. "You've got a Business Administration degree and a couple of Human Resources certifications. Can't see you using those here in Boring. Will you move to Charlottesville or Harrisonburg? Maybe Richmond?"

Me? I hadn't thought of my own future. I certainly didn't want to leave my family and my hometown. No way. "I don't know. Maybe Guthrie can give me some hours at the bookstore while I figure it out." Guthrie Armstrong owned Guthrie's Bookstore and lived over the shop. I'd been helping him because Guthrie hated his computer. He was the epitome of the older Southern Gentleman and had made his money during pre-internet days in the antiquarian book business. He still had book collectors who relied on him. And he was devoted to Aunt Adeline.

Neil put down his coffee and looked at each of us in turn. "The fact is there's not a lot of ways for the people of Boring to earn a living now. With the plant closing, Mayor Buckalew might be able to push through the offer from Silas Dale of Dale Casino Resorts."

"I don't know," I said slowly. "Mayor Buckalew has been careful to remain neutral on the subject of the casino offer. He only cares about four things: gossip, getting reelected, his Buster's Big Size Pies business, and courting Aunt Adeline."

"Hmph," Aunt Adeline snorted. "Walter 'Buster' Buckalew IV is an old fool. If his granddaddy hadn't formed that pie company and passed it down to Buster, he wouldn't have a feather to fly with."

"It's the town manager, Coralie Bouchard, we have to worry about. She's the power behind the throne, so to speak," I said. Coralie's husband had died in a boating accident and had been considerate enough to leave her a millionaire. Now she had her sights set on being the next Mrs. Buckalew and considered Aunt Adeline the only thing standing in her way. Never mind that Aunt Adeline showed no romantic interest in the mayor.

"Whether it's Mayor Buckalew or Coralie Bouchard making the decision, Neil's right," Josie said. "Word is Silas Dale never takes no for an answer. He talks enough for four sets of teeth. His people have made some big promises, if you catch my drift."

"Money under the table," Hugo said.

"And the promise to put Buster's Big Size Pies in vending machines throughout the casino resort," Josie said, raising her eyebrows and nodding.

"Never be able to fight it," Bobby declared, butter dribbling down his chin.

"Poppycock!" Aunt Adeline proclaimed. "The casino is an option that is not *on* the table of options. Our family's ancestors founded this town and Silas Dale and his cronies from New Jersey are not going to take it down with his gaudy, odious, revolting casino."

My fingers found my necklace, and I clasped Jane's gold silhouette.

"There are people in town that are in favor of the casino. The bottling plant closing could be what tips the scales in Silas Dale's favor. When money changes hands, when jobs are scarce...." Hugo spread his hands in a diplomatic gesture. "I'm not saying it's what I want for Boring."

Josie stabbed toast crumbs on her plate with the tips of her fingers. "Those casino people will come in here and ruin everything, our town, our way of life."

"Exactly," Aunt Adeline agreed. "The massive complex they're planning will clog local traffic all over the area, destroy the countryside, and irrevocably change not only Boring but neighboring towns as well."

"In addition to the hundred acres he already owns, Silas Dale's trying to buy those thirty acres of land near the bottling plant from the Oakley family," Neil said. "He hasn't gotten anywhere so far, but as Josie said, the man does not accept defeat."

"You're quiet, Kay. Trying to get inspiration from Jane?" Hugo said pointing at my Austen necklace.

Actually, I had been. As an idea came together in my mind, I felt the obstinate, headstrong girl in me rise up. I looked around the table at my family, my heart beating fast, my face beaming. "Yes, I did get inspiration from Jane. She's the solution to our town's troubles, everyone. Jane Austen will save Boring!"

Chapter Two

Hugo reached across the table and patted my hand. "Kay, you had a shock on Friday. You should take it easy. Get some rest."

"Silence, young man," Aunt Adeline admonished. "Kay, tell us your idea."

I looked at my family members. "In England, Australia, and across America there are Jane Austen Festivals. This December marks the 250th anniversary of Jane's birth. We could have a ticketed Jane Austen Festival, a happy, fun, celebration of Jane's life and the Janeites who love her. The whole town could be involved, using their skills and businesses to be a part of the festival and to make money. If we marketed it right, we could have Janeites from all over the eastern seaboard attend. Maybe from all over the country."

Josie rolled her eyes. Bobby shook his head. Neil rubbed his chin, deep in thought. Hugo's lips twisted into a grin.

Aunt Adeline's eyes glowed. "Oh, that would be wonderful! I'm on the board of The Jane Austen Guild of America. I could get the word out nationally," Aunt Adeline said. "We'd need a social media campaign."

"As a fellow Janeite, Hayley would love to handle that. Let's see, we'd have display tents up and down Main Street where people could sell Regency or Jane related items, a Promenade, archery lessons—"

"A musicale, screenings of the film adaptations," Aunt Adeline said. "You could teach people how to play Regency card games, Kay. And we must have a Proposal Booth where, for the price of a ticket, a Regency gentleman would propose marriage to you!"

"Not just any Regency gentleman," I said. "Mr. Darcy."

Aunt Adeline and I laughed.

"Oh, and the whole festival would culminate in a Regency Ball on Jane's birthday, December 16th," I said with certainty.

"Of course it would," Hugo murmured.

"There'd be carriage rides, horseback riding lessons," I said to him. "You could be in charge of that."

"Only if I could wear a top hat."

"You'd definitely wear a top hat," I told him. "We'd need to put everything together, get organized." I looked around the table. "Come on, everyone, we can do it! We've got over three months. And don't forget that a couple of summers ago we had that massive Jane Austen readathon across town and everyone fell in love with Jane. We'll get support."

"Maybe by the time of the festival, I'd be done renovating the cabins," Josie mused. "Some festival attendees could stay at the Lake. The Farmhouse Restaurant and Inn would benefit too."

"I'd give the festival plenty of coverage in the newspaper. With an influx of visitors, all the local businesses would profit. I think the idea has potential, Kay," Neil said. "We'd need to have a town meeting with the mayor fast before they make a move with Silas Dale. Now that the bottling plant is closed, time is critical."

"We have a meeting scheduled for three o'clock," Aunt Adeline said. "Now that we have our plan to save Boring, we need plenty of business people to attend the meeting, get on board and see how they can make a profit."

Everyone turned to look at her. "Today? At three o'clock?" I asked.

She shrugged. "I knew we'd come up with a plan to save Boring, and I wanted to present it today."

"You've had a busy morning," Josie said.

"Morning? I set it up over the weekend," Aunt Adeline corrected. "You know how Coralie Bouchard is with her mint juleps in the summer. I know precisely the time when she's had two and is on her third."

"You're the greatest, Aunt Adeline," I said and wondered for the millionth time what I'd do without her. "Let's get this presentation ready to go. Hugo, can you and Neil make phone calls to business owners and get them excited?"

"On it," Neil said, pulling out his cell.

Hugo nodded his agreement and stood. "I'll run over to the Golden Age Diner and talk up the festival. Breakfast there is the epicenter of town gossip. Word will spread fast."

He and Neil left, Neil talking fast on his cell.

"Josie," Aunt Adeline said. "I want you to stay and help Kay and myself. And, Bobby, I want to speak with you privately about

Starling Grocery and the workers who've lost their jobs. That idea I've been cogitating over is about ready."

I wondered what scheme she had in mind. There was no time to find out as Aunt Adeline spoke to Bobby alone in the living room while Josie and I cleared the table. After Bobby left, Josie, Aunt Adeline and I put our heads together and worked on the presentation for the town council. Two hours later, I'd hardly caught my breath when I heard the sound of the back door opening and Guthrie's voice.

"Kay and Josie, I'll see you both at the town hall," Aunt Adeline said rushing from the room. "Guthrie! Just the man I want to see."

Josie gave me a quick hug. "You're a clever girl, sis. I'm proud of you," she said before leaving.

I stood in the center of the kitchen smiling at her words, then pulled myself to order.

Having missed my morning run three days in a row while wallowing in self-pity, I decided to walk briskly to Hayley's Bakery on Main Street. The bakery wasn't that far from the end of our long driveway, but still. I could burn off a few calories with this heat. At ninety-two degrees, outside felt like a steam bath. We'd get a thunderstorm in the afternoon, but it wouldn't cool things off. Oh no. It would only make the air more humid.

Founded in 1778 by Samuel Boring, landowner, and the Starling brothers, who were wealthy English merchants, Boring was a typical small town, with a business section covering several blocks of Main Street and tree-lined residential streets fanning off from Main Street in all directions. Main Street was a mix of converted red brick, pastel clapboard, and stone buildings, which housed businesses, with living spaces conveniently located above. The big Village Green, a grassy rectangle near the end of Starling Farm's driveway, served as a town square. Starling Grocery, situated at the very end of town past the railroad tracks, was one of the only modernish buildings having been built in 1955. The other was the Golden Age Diner, built in the 1970s. The Blue Ridge Mountains to the west rose up like a group of earthen soldiers dressed in summer's green.

Hardly anyone was outside, but I waved to Mimi Monday who hurried from the direction of the Golden Age Diner, grey curls bouncing, toward Monday's Country Store. She returned the greeting but didn't stop. I smiled to myself. Hugo had worked fast. Mimi was Mayor Buckalew's equal when it came to town gossip and probably wanted to tell customers at the store the news.

I crossed the Village Green where a "Don't Pass the Buckalew!" sign from the mayor's last campaign was fading in the sun. I was glad to cross the sweltering, cobblestone street and the red brick sidewalk to Hayley's Bakery. The bakery was a pink clapboard building with hanging pots of pink and purple petunias below the shop's sign, which was in the shape of a cupcake.

Out of the September heat and into the freezing air condition-ing of the bakery, I breathed in the scent of coffee and sugar. The morning rush was over. My bestie, Hayley Conner, was waiting on Betsy Bell Ward, owner of the town's fabric store, Happy Fabrics.

"What about a root beer, Betsy Bell?" Hayley asked reaching into the cold case. She had on tan shorts and pink tee shirt that said "Hayley's Bakery" inside the outline of a cupcake.

"I don't know if I've had one of those," Betsy Bell, a petite blonde in peach-colored jeans and a white top with a ruffled neck-line, said in her soft, gentle voice. "There's no alcohol in it, right?"

"No, hon. Like ginger ale, there's no alcohol." Hayley shot me a grin and tossed her wild lion's mane of tight brown and gold curly hair. She always says that, since she's a Leo, it's the way she has to wear her natural hair.

"Good morning, Kay." Betsy Bell smiled at me. "Hayley's help-ing me pick out a new soda to drink now that, well, *you know*. I al-ways have one soda a day, with lunch. Orange juice with breakfast, a soda with lunch, and water with dinner."

Betsy Bell was about the sweetest woman in town, but she was timid to a fault. I'd been trying to think of a way to help bring her out of her shell, but hadn't succeeded yet. "A root beer sounds refreshing."

Betsy Bell peered at the bottle in Hayley's hand. "There's no caffeine in it, is there? Caffeine riles me so."

Hayley and I exchanged a look. Who could imagine Betsy Bell riled?

"There's no caffeine," Hayley assured her pressing the bottle into her hands. "You take that now, on the house. Let me know if you like it. We'll find something else if you don't."

"Thank you, Hayley. I appreciate it. I have to watch my pennies. People may not be buying fabrics right now since, well, *you know*."

Hayley and I nodded as she turned to go.

I put my hand on her shoulder. "Betsy Bell, there's going to be a meeting at three o'clock at the town hall about the future of Boring. Aunt Adeline and I want to present a plan so that everyone doesn't think the casino is our only option. As a business owner, you'll be needed. Can you make it?"

Betsy Bell held the bottle of root beer close to her chest. She looked outside and gazed skyward. "I'd rather lick the sun than see those casino people destroy our town." She turned to me, a surprisingly steely glint in her eyes. "Gambling isn't a very nice pastime. Of course I'll be there."

She marched outside.

"Whoa," I said to Hayley.

"The girl's got some gumption after all." Hayley said. "So, what's the plan?"

"Jane Austen is going to save our town," I said, pulling my cell phone out of my dress pocket.

"Cool. Are you calling her now? Is she coming to the town meeting? Bringing Mr. Darcy, I hope?"

At my frown, she said, "You know I had an ex during that brief time I lived in New York City who asked me if Jane Austen was one of my friends. I guess since I talk about her a lot. Good Lord, he was dumb as a box of rocks."

I scrolled through the notes I'd taken this morning and filled Hayley in on what Aunt Adeline and I had figured out about the Jane Austen Festival so far.

Hayley, a true Janeite, grew more excited as we talked about the events culminating in a Regency Ball for Jane Austen's 250th birthday. "I have *Martha Lloyd's Household* book which has recipes, in addition to all the Regency era recipes I've collected over the years. I could make apricot tarts, syllabub, gingerbread, seed cakes, shortbread, Bath buns, plum cake, scones, mince pies."

I grinned. "Sounds delicious. What about your mom? Do you think Serenity would have time to do Regency silhouettes during the festival?"

"Oh yeah. She'd love it. Something different from her paintings. She loves Austen too you know."

At that moment, Valeria Garcia, otherwise known as Dessert Decorator Extraordinaire, walked into the shopfront from the back carrying a large tray of cupcakes. She slid them into the main case. I noticed today's winged eyeliner color was bright green like the grass in Dogwood Park. "Hey girls, I know you love these. I had some time this morning so I made them."

Extra-thick, pale, blue frosting covered each of two dozen cupcakes. A miniature *Pride and Prejudice* fondant book cover had been placed on top of each one. "Oh, yum! They look decadent, Valeria," I said, pushing thoughts of my missed runs out of my mind.

Hayley said, "Hey, Valeria, would you be up to creating a giant 250th birthday cake for Jane Austen? I'll tell you the plan later."

"For my girl, Jane? You know I will. Lemme think. Six tiers for her six great novels. Mr. Darcy, Mr. Knightly, Mr. Tilney, and all her other boys represented. My mouth is watering just thinking about it."

"Uh-huh. Your mouth is not watering for just the cake," Hayley teased.

We all laughed and I said, "You're the best, Valeria."

Valeria waved a hand in acknowledgement as she sashayed back to the kitchen. She would have tossed her waist-length dark hair had it not been pinned up and confined to a hairnet.

"How does she do it?" I asked gazing at the blue confections. "Look at the detail on the book cover. They're perfect."

Hayley pulled a cupcake out and handed it to me. "She never had any formal training. Her mama taught her. The rest is pure imagination."

I could only nod as I stuffed a big bite of cupcake into my mouth.

The bell rang over the door. I hoped it was another friend since I probably looked like I'd smashed my face headfirst into blue frosting.

A tall, lean man with broad shoulders, slim hips, and dark brown hair entered. His eyes were blue-gray. I didn't have to work in the men's department of Brooks Brothers to know his dark blue suit was expensive and immaculately cut.

For my ears only Hayley whispered. "Mmmm. First impressions are favorable." She cleared her throat, then said brightly, "Morning. What can I get you?"

"A large coffee, please. Black," he said in a posh English accent.

"Coming up." She gawked at him for a moment, then stepped to the coffee machine.

He looked at me and to my shame, I felt myself blush. I wasn't the type who fell for a guy's looks. Even when they had hair that had a sexy wave to it and curled at the ends. The sexy English accent was the icing on top.

Um, icing...My mouth full of cupcake and my lips coated with frosting, I nodded at him awkwardly. Mary Bennet would have had more grace.

Without acknowledging the nod, he turned back to Hayley.

Over the whirr of the coffee machine, he said, "Is there a Walgreens nearby?"

"Not from around here, are you?" Hayley said with a smile. "Mr. Bexley's Pharmacy is across the street and nine doors down."

I was chewing as fast as I could.

Hayley picked up on my embarrassment and slid me a fistful of napkins and the stranger his coffee. "Will that be all? How about a cupcake to go with your coffee?" she asked, indicating the fresh tray of *Pride and Prejudice* treats.

The stranger glanced at the cupcakes. Without a trace of humor in his voice, he said, "They are tolerable but not handsome enough to tempt me."

What? Did he just use Austen to insult those cupcakes? Luckily, I had a napkin over my mouth so I'm pretty sure he missed my outraged gasp. Also luckily, I didn't choke on cupcake crumbs.

Hayley cut me a look; her eyes filled with disbelief.

After he ran his card through the card reader, the stranger said a clipped "Thanks for the offer. Too much sugar for me." He picked up his coffee and walked out the door without looking at me again or saying where he was from.

The bell was still jangling when I leaned against the bakery case and said, "Too much sugar? What does he want? A cupcake without frosting?"

"That would be like eating sadness," Hayley said. "He's probably some kind of health nut. He was so hot though, I'm gonna forgive him. Did you see those piercing blue eyes? Bet you he's a Scorpio."

"Never mind his star sign. What if he's one of the casino people? And was he being sarcastic the way he made that 'tolerable' remark?"

Hayley shrugged and handed me a bottle of cold water. "It's a famous line from *Pride and Prejudice*. He had an English accent; he's probably from England. Jane's on their money over there. He could even be a male Janeite."

"I doubt that," I said and took a long drink.

"I'd be happy to convert him," Hayley said, waggling her eyebrows and twirling a piece of her curly hair. "The two of us on my comfy sofa, cups of Earl Grey in hand, me reading to him. As long as Jane Pawsten keeps her claws to herself. She's picky about my friends and her good opinion, once lost, is gone forever."

We burst out laughing. When I recovered, I said, "Remember what Aunt Adeline always says: 'Men are a dime a dozen but one's cat is priceless.'"

"Truth!"

"What about your own handsome guy? Detective Derek Gordon? With the slightest encouragement from you, he'd be at the jewelry store shopping for a solitaire."

Hayley's face fell. "He knows better than to waste his time. We're just friends, Kay. You need to understand that. I don't want to get married."

Didn't want to get married! This was sudden. Ever since we were little Hayley had dreamed of finding her true love. Had she had a fight with Derek? Had I overestimated their attachment? "Every Jane Austen heroine wants to get married," I reminded her, disregarding the fact that women in Regency England *had* to marry to have a roof over their heads since, generally, they couldn't have careers.

"Kay, we're not in a book. This is real life."

"Yeah. That's true. You're right." I backed off fast. I couldn't lecture her. I hadn't thought of marriage since my college guy—I'm not going to call him my college sweetheart because he wasn't—noped out of Boring, our relationship, the whole settling down thing. I tossed the remaining crumbs of my cupcake into the trash and checked the time on my phone. "I'd better go. There's so much to do."

I turned to go and looked back over my shoulder. "I'll see you at the town meeting. Sit with me."

"Sure thing. Hey, is Hugo back from Middleburg? I thought I saw his Tacoma."

"He is. Came home without Mitzi, thank goodness. I didn't like her or the way she treated Hugo." I turned and walked to the door but heard Hayley mutter, "Without Mitzi. That's a shame."

Chapter Three

Housed inside the three-story rectangular, sandstone Municipal building and smelling like old pencil shavings and eraser crumbs, the town hall was packed. Not only were the rows of chairs filled, but people were standing three-deep against the walls. Hayley had saved me a seat in the second row behind Neil, Josie, and Hugo. Sheriff Bud Wilkinson, his deputies, and Detective Derek Gordon scanned the crowd as if expecting trouble. I recognized almost everyone there and felt guilt wash over me as folks from the bottling plant smiled and nodded at me. Betsy Bell gave me a shy finger wave.

At the front of the room, on the stage, stood a long table, flanked by a standing Virginia flag and a United States flag. In seats facing the crowd, were; Mayor Buckalew, Coralie Bouchard, Mr. Fulton from the bank, Josie's husband, Bobby, two men I didn't recognize, and, yes there he was, the stranger from Hayley's bakery. He must be part of the casino contingent.

Ceiling fans droned above, but they couldn't cut the tension in the air.

There was a commotion in the back of the room. I turned to see Aunt Adeline, dressed in a bright yellow Regency gown, gliding up the aisle greeting people. She took a minute to smile and shake hands with Mr. Oakley.

She's bought that land out from under Silas Dale. Strike One.

I thought proudly that she had a regal air about her, and it wasn't because of the Regency attire and sprinkle of Austen-speak. Instead, it was in her mannerisms, the way she walked, her smile, the way she made people feel. She was the epitome of the Southern matriarch.

She stopped when she reached us. Neil, Josie, Hugo, and Hayley gave her their attention.

"Everyone's here," she said in a low voice. "All of you did a superb job getting the word out. I'll make the presentation. Look for opportunities to support me if it comes to that. You too, Hayley. Is your mother here? I don't see her."

"Yes, ma'am. In the peacock caftan by Mr. and Mrs. Monday."

"Good." She searched the crowd then waved at Hayley's mother.

"Aunt Adeline," I whispered. "Who is the man on stage in the dark blue suit?"

She smiled. "The criminally handsome one? That's Flynn Holden. You've heard of the Holdens, Kay. They're big in investment banking here in the States and across the pond. Flynn's uncle, Pete Holden, died recently, leaving Flynn his house and vineyard and our community center. I think Flynn's been down in Williamsburg," she said speculatively. "Had I known he was in town, I'd have invited him to breakfast this morning."

Not one of the casino people, then.

Aunt Adeline's gaze met Mayor Buckalew's. "Oh, Buster knows he's in for it. I've got to take my place. Kay, come with me."

"What?" I said, panic rising.

"Right now," she said, taking my arm. "It's your idea, and I need your enthusiasm."

She marched me up the steps to the table, pulled out two chairs, and we sat down. My heart pounded in my chest.

Coralie Bouchard made a habit of dressing in coral colors. Today, she wore a coral-colored linen, shift dress. She glared at Aunt Adeline, then turned a cloying smile on Mayor Buckalew and gave him a gentle nudge.

The mayor struggled out of his chair and shrugged on his navy-blue blazer with the Buster's Big Size Pies logo on the breast pocket. He tapped his microphone. "Good afternoon, everybody. We've got a big decision to make today, so let's get to it. First, I'll introduce our guests. To my left is Silas Dale, the owner and chief executive officer of Dale Casino Resorts. And next to Mr. Dale is Jonathan Warren, his vice president."

While Jonathan Warren, in his thirties, had a boyish charm and a big smile that revealed dimples, Silas Dale, in his sixties, observed the crowd like a copperhead ready to strike. His black eyes were expressionless, his dyed auburn hair failed to cover his balding head, his cheeks and nose were a bright pink, and his mouth was wet.

A murmur went through the crowd. Hostile faces mixed with curious gazes.

The mayor wiped his brow. "Oh, my wits have gone begging. We also have a very welcome newcomer to Boring, one who I invited personally to join us. Mr. Flynn Holden from Holden Investment Partners. Flynn recently suffered the loss of his uncle, Pete Holden who y'all knew."

The mayor introduced everyone around the table to the casino people and Flynn Holden. The latter spared me the briefest of glances but I heard him mutter, "The girl with the Jane Austen cupcake."

It soon became clear that the mayor had assumed that, with the closing of the Hurdee Gurdee bottling plant, the casino project would go ahead. He allowed Silas Dale to reiterate how the casino would benefit the town and bring it "into the modern age." Dale spoke down to the people as if they were uneducated peasants. I saw people crossing their arms over their chests and pursing their lips.

Aunt Adeline politely interrupted. "Excuse me, my niece, Kay Starling, and I would like to present the town with another option so that no one feels pressured to do anything that would irrevocably change our way of life. But before we begin, my nephew-in-law, Bobby Rice, has an announcement."

I looked curiously at Bobby.

He stood and spoke into a microphone, "At Starling Grocery, we're concerned about our neighbors who've lost their employment due to the bottling plant closure. Therefore, if you show your last pay-stub from Hurdee Gurdee at the cash register, for the next two months your groceries are free. You'll be getting an email with all the particulars shortly." He sat down.

My jaw dropped.

Loud cheers, whoops of delight, and applause broke out in the room. The mood changed to one of hope.

Cranky old Sheriff Bud Wilkinson covered his microphone and leveled his gaze at Silas Dale. "We take care of our own here. I don't need people from New Jersey to tell me what to do about our town."

Silas Dale's eyes shot laser beams of hate in the Sheriff's direction.

Aunt Adeline lowered her head toward me and whispered, "You have the ex-employees' email addresses, right?"

I kept my voice low. I knew Aunt Adeline was wealthy, but still. "Yes, I have their addresses, but how on earth did you work this out? Do you realize how many people are involved?"

She straightened. "Of course I know. I've already transferred the money to the grocery store account." I had no time to wonder at her having this much ready cash, because Aunt Adeline and I quickly laid out our plan for the Jane Austen Festival and 250th Birthday Party to the attentive crowd. A rousing discussion ensued where various business owners, including Hayley, spoke out about how they could play a part, bring in more of the townspeople, and everyone would benefit in the scheme. This prompted a flurry of people to weigh in and throw out their own money-making ideas.

The town manager banged on the table for quiet.

Coralie fixed me with a hard look. "You can separate fantasy from reality, can't you, Miss Starling? You may be one of these so-called Janeites, but are there enough people interested in a long-dead author to merit this hare-brained project?"

My fingers went to my Jane necklace. "Jane Austen is one of the most celebrated writers in the English language. It will be her 250th birthday. She's internationally famous and her books have been adapted for TV, films, and the theater. Her writing is timeless. Established Jane Austen Festivals attract thousands of people. Yes, there'll be lots of interest."

Jonathan Warren spoke up in a Texas drawl. "Y'all can't expect many people here in Boring, Miz Starling. There's no guarantee of business. Whereas Dale Casino Resorts have been successful everywhere we've built our complexes. We'll be successful in Boring. You can bet on it." Out came those dimples again as he grinned, his eyes lingering on me.

A sprinkle of laughter met his *bon mot*, but it seemed clear that with the promise of free groceries and another way to make money other than destroying the town as they knew it, the casino people had lost the crowd.

Strike Two.

Silas Dale perceived the way the crowd was leaning if the sour expression on his sagging face meant anything.

Flynn Holden reached for a microphone and rose to his feet with languid ease and perfect posture. All eyes gravitated toward him. "I know Jane Austen's popularity. I read one of her novels in my schooldays. I can see the potential in the ideas the Starling family have put forth. Although I was born and raised in England, besides my family's investment business, my interests lie in American history. I've worked for Colonial Williamsburg. Mr. Dale, for those who don't know, Colonial Williamsburg is the country's largest living history museum. It's an immersive, authentic, 18th century experience. I believe my knowledge and connections from my Colonial Williamsburg experience could benefit a Jane Austen Festival." He looked out over the crowd. "The Holden family will assist the Starlings in financial matters in regards to the festival as well."

Not just a handsome face then.

I stood, brimming with excitement and addressed the crowd. "If—no, *when* the Jane Austen Festival is a success, we could work toward becoming a destination attraction like Colonial Williamsburg, only on a much smaller scale. We could transform our future, our children's future. Let's change the name of our town from Boring to Jane Austen Town and get started!"

A big burst of applause met my words. Happiness washed over me. Aunt Adeline pressed my hand in approval. Flynn Holden looked at me and gave me a slight nod.

Wait, did this mean I would be working with a man who didn't like cupcakes?

Mayor Buckalew finally called for order; his gaze locked on Aunt Adeline's. "Maybe one day our town could be as fortunate as Colonial Williamsburg. For now, let's start with the festival. For the foreseeable future, I hereby declare Boring to be re-named Jane Austen Town."

Amid the cheers that followed this statement, Silas Dale stood, grabbed his microphone, and cut his hand through the air, silencing everyone. "You'll regret this and come crawling back to me, all of you!" he snarled. "You women bribed these people with your free groceries but it won't last!" He looked at the mayor. "Call me when you've come to your senses."

Jonathan gave me a sheepish look, hesitated as if he wanted to speak to me, but then left with his boss.

Strike three.

Aunt Adeline gave me a warm smile. "I'm proud of you, Kay." She chuckled, then whispered, "Did you see the way Jonathan Warren couldn't take his eyes off you? Like he could eat you up with a spoon."

"He's good looking and successful, but he's also the enemy."

Several people wanted to talk to me but my head was spinning with thoughts and my heart was filled with emotion. A planning committee formed and agreed to meet the next day.

I excused myself and ran outside. There was something I urgently had to check.

The heavens had opened up. Rain poured down and thunder cracked overhead. I ran and ran down the redbrick sidewalks, smelling fried chicken from the Golden Age Diner, past the cozy shops and storefronts on Main Street, down the long driveway until I reached Starling Farm. Inside the house, I kicked off my soaking wet tennis shoes and then rushed to the antique barrister bookcase in the library.

With trembling fingers, I raised the glass door on the top shelf. I looked at Aunt Adeline's cherished collection of Jane Austen's books. Tears sprang to my eyes and ran down my cheeks as I saw the gap where her first edition of *Sense and Sensibility*, published in 1811 by Thomas Egerton and passed down from Aunt Adeline's great, great grandmother, had been. I remembered that a few years back, a copy had sold at a New York auction for $100,000.

Aunt Adeline had sold—likely Guthrie had done it for her—a treasured family heirloom to help cover the emergency groceries for those now unemployed.

"I *must* make the Jane Austen Festival a success for our town," I said to the empty room. "Aunt Adeline believes in me. I can't let her down. Nothing must go wrong. *Nothing*."

At that moment, a flash of lightning illuminated the room followed by a clap of thunder that shook the ground.

Chapter Four

On Thursday, December 11, I picked up my already bulging pineapple-shaped reticule and shoved my cell phone inside. It was a bigger purse than they used in Austen's time, but I'd learned over the past three months that striving for historical accuracy was one thing, but achieving it for a public event in the 21st century was another.

The day was bright and sunny with temperatures in the fifties. Our part of Virginia tended to have mild winters, although we did experience the occasional arctic blast, usually in January and February. I'd already fed my outdoor friends, including Tilney, the mischievous crow who'd brought me a shiny piece of foil, an upgrade from the Hurdee Gurdee bottle cap.

Clad in a long-sleeved, brown floral, Regency Day gown, based on the one Emma wore in the 2009 adaptation and stitched by Betsy Bell, I joined Aunt Adeline, who wore dark green and had a gold and green paisley shawl about her shoulders, on the front steps. "Neil's at the newspaper but where's Hugo?" she asked. "He'd better not still be asleep."

"I'll text him."

"Text who?" Hugo said appearing from around the side of the house and making me jump.

"You. We were worried you were still asleep," I told him.

"Seriously? I've been up since five taking care of the horses," he said and yawned. He wore jeans and a gray, cable knit sweater with his tall top hat. He'd become ridiculously attached to the thing since purchasing it in a costume shop in Harrisonburg.

"Come on, you two. We don't want to be late for the meeting. The festival starts tomorrow!" Aunt Adeline said.

We walked to Guthrie's Books. On the way, I admired the royal blue banner with a silver-colored silhouette of Austen that read "JANE AUSTEN FESTIVAL AND 250TH BIRTHDAY CELEBRATION December 12-16" hanging across Main Street. In smaller letters underneath was the hashtag: #PartyLikeIts1811. All down Main Street, pole banners attached to our Victorian-styled street lamps featured the iconic likeness of Jane Austen in her pale blue dress with the hashtag underneath. Bobby knew someone who did pennants, and the planning committee had decided on the simple design. Dotted down Main Street were rows of white rental tents with people erecting more. Main Street was closed to vehicle traffic for the duration of the festival.

The town bustled with activity, but sadly, some people had left for employment in the cities. There were empty storefronts. An expensive dress shop, an antique shop, and French restaurant that, while the food had been good, the prices had made it special occasion only, all closed.

Guthrie's Books was a brick building with parchment-colored shutters. A display of Jane Austen books of various editions and prices took up the front window.

Hayley's Bakery was next door to Guthrie's. Heading our way, Hayley wore jeans and a long-sleeved black tee shirt that depicted a rolling pin and the words, "This Is How I Roll." She juggled a cardboard container of six coffees while clutching a pink bakery box. An iPad shoulder bag crisscrossed her chest.

Hugo jogged the few steps to meet her. "Hey, Hailstorm, I'll carry the coffee."

Hayley put her head to one side and slitted her eyes. "Really, Hugo? I was six years old."

He took the container and chuckled. "Let's go. I need this coffee."

Hayley glared at his retreating back. I felt a smile starting at the memory of the schoolyard altercation involving snowballs made of hail that resulted in the nickname, but redirected my thoughts back to the festival.

The intoxicating smell of books hit me as we entered Guthrie's shop. We headed to a conference table at the back of the store. I smiled at yet another big display of Austen's books but flinched when I saw the sign that read "Ask About Collectible Editions." Aunt Adeline's copy of *Sense and Sensibility* was probably long gone. Guthrie kept a network of collectors all over the country despite loathing his computer and the internet.

Guthrie Armstrong, seventy years old with a head of thick gray hair, a full mustache, and an endearing smile for Aunt Adeline, greeted us and we settled with our coffee around the table.

Flynn, in a blue collared Oxford shirt and dark jeans, accepted coffee from Hayley, but declined her offer of a freshly-made apple fritter, continuing his War on Sugar. We'd clashed on many things while planning the festival. He had decided opinions, could be aloof, but he was also reliable, intelligent, and had been generous with his money in regards to the festival's needs. I was determined to start things off in a positive way this morning.

"Flynn, I see the white rental tents are a big hit. Thanks again for donating them." I tried for a smile but suspect I grimaced. "Is the militia ready for their appearance at the opening Promenade?"

"Yes," he answered me but addressed everyone. "Through my Colonial Williamsburg contacts, we've two dozen men of all ages fitted out in red coats and white breeches. Besides leading the Promenade tomorrow afternoon, they'll be out and about during festival events."

"Two women are included, right?" I asked.

He didn't roll his eyes, but there was an eyeroll in his tone of voice. "Yes, Kay, I told you there would be." He looked around the table. "Kay put aside her rule about historical accuracy in this instance in favor of equality."

"Something Austen would have appreciated," I said quietly.

Aunt Adeline spoke up. "As I understand it, lodging in town and the surrounding areas is completely full. The Farmhouse Inn,

Starling Cabins at the Lake, the Roadside Beds Motor Court, and all the hotels and motels east of Harrisonburg are booked."

Guthrie gave her an admiring smile. "That's right, Addy. In addition, families have rented out extra bedrooms to festival attendees. People have been clever about bringing in extra income."

A gray cat with yellow eyes, who Guthrie called The Little Gray Animal, wound his way around my ankles under the table. I reached down to pet his soft fur and felt him purr.

Hayley had her iPad open. "Social media checking in here. I've updated our website, Facebook page, TikTok, and Instagram accounts using the hashtag #PartyLikeIts1811."

"Our YouTube channel is the best," Hugo said and polished off the last bite of his apple fritter. "You and Aunt Adeline demonstrating recipes made in Jane Austen's time was a stroke of genius if I say so myself."

Hayley clucked her tongue. "It was *my* idea, not yours."

Hugo pointed with his coffee cup. "I suggested you dress in Regency clothes."

"You both nicked that idea from the English Heritage channel with the Victorian cook, Mrs. Crocombe," Flynn said.

Must he? Did he have to be such a stick in the mud?

"Whatever," Hugo shrugged. "It's getting thousands of views."

For the next two hours, we went over the list of day-by-day festival events. When we got to the Regency Dance Workshop, I looked up. "I haven't met Nathaniel Playford yet. He's teaching English country dances, isn't he?"

Flynn nodded. "He started with the locals last Friday when he got to town."

"He already has a reputation," Hayley said, shaking her head. "Made a vulgar remark about my fruit tarts."

My eyes narrowed. "What? That's disgusting."

"Sorry, Hayley. He's a bit of a character," Flynn acknowledged. "But we are lucky to have him. He's done English country dancing lessons up and down the East Coast."

Guthrie raised a bushy eyebrow at him. "The man sounds as appealing as an angry wasp. No *gentleman* would make such a remark to Hayley."

"Hayley, what more have you heard?" I asked before Flynn could respond.

"I went to Monday's Country Store for some disposable plates and to see Mama's finished painting."

Aunt Adeline said, "Serenity did masterful work covering up the Hurdee Gurdee advertisement on the side of the building with a beautiful likeness of Jane Austen. The whole town owes her a debt of gratitude. She still plans to set up her own tent and do silhouettes, correct, Hayley?"

"Thank you, and yes ma'am, she will. So back to Nathaniel Playford. Y'all know Mimi Monday likes to gossip."

All of us except Flynn nodded.

"She told me that Playford is quite the flirt, and some of the ladies take it seriously. He took Francie out for dinner last night."

Francie Perkins, along with her grandmother, Miss June, owned the Golden Age Diner.

Hugo scoffed. "Francie is a great girl, but no man is going to marry her when they know bossy, know-it-all, Miss June comes with the bargain. Anyway, Francie's in love with all those Golden Age movie stars."

Aunt Adeline threw a side-eye at Hugo that silenced him. "Miss June is eighty-one years old and deserves your respect."

"Yes, ma'am," Hugo muttered.

Hayley continued. "Mimi said there's a woman named Alexandra Bartholomew staying at the Farmhouse Inn. Alexandra owns a B&B in Massachusetts. Evidently, she puts on Jane Austen-themed weekends. Nathaniel Playford was with *her* Tuesday night. Mimi implied they were as close as hamburgers and French fries."

"So what? He's single, isn't he? Don't be such a prude," Hugo griped.

"Have you met him, Hugo?" I asked.

"He was over at Gator's last night when I stopped in for a beer. Must have been after his date with Francie. We got to talking about east coast beaches," Hugo replied. "He likes a place with a year-round beach. Seemed full of himself and, um, focused on the ladies."

"Exactly what I've heard," Flynn said. "He's a performer of sorts. You know what that lot are like."

"Hayley's right to be concerned, though," Aunt Adeline said. "We don't want trouble of any sort. Mr. Playford sounds like a cad. Someone needs to put a flea in his ear."

"I'm the person to do that. I'll visit him today," I said. All we needed was for the dancing master to cause disgrace to fall on the festival, and my hopes for our town would wither away like snow under an unforgiving sun.

Flynn sighed. "Very well, Kay. But don't call him Nate. He insists on going by Nathaniel. And don't make him cross. He has an artistic temperament. Remember, we need him for the next six days."

Aunt Adeline fixed Flynn with a look. "I'm certain Kay will do just as she ought."

Flynn glanced at the time on his phone. "If you leave now, you can have a word with him after his morning lesson ends."

"That's just what I'll do," I told him, immediately gathering my things and saying my goodbyes.

I welcomed the cool air on my face when I stepped outside. Main Street was a veritable hive of activity. I headed in the direction of the community center multi-purpose room, which had been dubbed The Assembly Rooms for the festival.

At the Village Green, I waved to Bobby, Eric Longo, and Tyler Carter, our fire chief who had his dalmatian, Lucky, with him. The men were noisily constructing a wooden platform. I caught the whiff of an earthy, pine scent. Alongside their working area lay a tall Balsam Fir still wrapped tightly. Not something Jane Austen would have had at Chawton Cottage, but we had decided people would expect a Christmas tree this close to Christmas.

Eric's wife, Lorraine, whose baby was due in three weeks, walked around with her clipboard checking off vendors who'd reserved a tent.

Josie's daughter, my niece Sarah Beth, ran across Main Street to Monday's Country Store, one hand on her head holding a navy-blue bonnet in place.

All the businesses on Main Street had worked together to decorate their storefronts with plenty of greenery. Tiny white lights wound their way through the boughs; again, not exactly historically accurate, but the little lights would be magical once the sun set.

I entered the community center and noticed how quiet it was. People were busy outside, but inside, the lower rooms used for art, yoga and other classes, were empty. I walked up the stairs to the Assembly Rooms. The soaring room, with a capacity for a significant amount of people, had brick interior walls and dark hardwood floors. A raised area at one end would serve as the Musician's Gallery the night of the ball.

The lively strains of a Scottish reel met my ears and made me smile. I stepped into the room as the music, which was coming from Bluetooth speakers connected to Nathaniel Playford's tablet, came to an end. Six couples, comprised of ladies dressed in a range of clothing from Regency gowns, to street clothes, to a leotard, caught their breath and fanned themselves. All except the lady in a black leotard who had a face like thunder.

Nathaniel Playford was a somewhat stocky man of average height in his late forties dressed in Regency clothing. His cotton lawn shirt was tucked into a pair of skin-tight, revealing, tan-colored knee breeches. He wore white stockings and black dancing shoes. His sandy-colored hair was on the long side and unruly. A wayward lock fell across his forehead, and he kept tossing his head back as if that would arrange it.

His loud, clear voice held a smirk in it. "That's all for today, my dearest turtledoves. Come and see me at any time with questions or if you want to be privately tutored. And if your calves are sore, I have strong hands."

A few of the ladies tittered and blushed.

A sick feeling welled in my stomach like the time I saw a greasy bacon sandwich in the gutter during an afternoon rainstorm.

Nathaniel ignored me and instead snapped his fingers at the slim woman wearing a leotard. She was in her early fifties with long, straight blonde hair. Her face was covered in what looked like an entire makeup counter worth of cosmetics.

"Alexandra! It is bad manners to walk through a set of dancers!"

So, this was the woman from the B&B in Massachusetts. She approached Nathaniel and hissed something in his ear. When she drew back, I could see her lips pursed into a thin line and her green eyes flashing.

He laughed at her.

She brushed past me as she made for the door. A cloud of J'adore, Dior's perfume, followed in her wake.

Nathaniel strolled to the table containing his tablet, some pamphlets, and a bottle of Hurdee Gurdee soda of all things! He took a swig of the drink and turned my way. "Yes?"

Now that we were alone, I steeled myself. "I'm Kay Starling, one of the people chairing the festival."

He tossed his head. "You're ecstatic to have me, I know, I know. Well, a new festival in such a small town is not normally my thing, but I'm doing it as a favor to Flynn Holden. The whole Jane Austen plan was his idea. Your town's about to go under."

Flynn's idea? I opened my mouth to correct him then remembered that to argue with a fool makes two. "I'm sure Flynn told you that we are hosting a *wholesome* event here in Jane Austen Town. Our town's future depends on the success of the festival. We wouldn't want any hurt feelings among the ladies, misunderstandings regarding intentions or, worse, a scandal. I'm sure you understand."

He let out a hearty laugh. "I'm beginning to," he said. He cocked his head. "You must be the town spinster. Not versed in the way of romance, poor thing."

How dare he? I took a step towards him and raised my chin. "I'm the person authorizing your paycheck. My advice to you is to back off the female festival attendees and the women in town. I've had reports of your behavior, and now I've seen it first-hand. It's offensive, demeaning, and completely unacceptable."

At my words, his face, which had been filled with amusement, gradually altered to scorn. "Do you know the dance, La Boulanger, Miss Starling?"

"Yes, but what has that to do with anything?"

He leaned down and got in my face. "It's a rowdy dance with many partners, and that's how I live my life. There's nothing wrong with that, something you might learn in time. I'm not changing my ways for your little town." He straightened. "Now, since you're in charge, you can get me candles. We have cande-labras, but no candles. Beeswax only. I must create the right at-mosphere for dancing. Candlelight brings romance!" He turned and strolled back to his tablet. Mozart filled the room. Nathaniel began humming along to the music and then he began waltzing with himself.

I could hardly believe my eyes. There was no reasoning with him.

"Vile, loathsome man! I could kill him." I texted Flynn as I walked out of the building and toward Monday's Country Store.

"Calm down. I'll walk up there and have a word with him now."

Oooh! I crammed my cell phone in my reticule. How dare Flynn tell me to calm down? Did he think he could make Nathaniel change his tune? Fine, let him try.

Monday's Country Store was a gray, clapboard, colonial-style house with a wide, wraparound porch cluttered antique milk cans, fresh wreaths sporting cherry red bows, small Christmas trees in galvanized buckets, and wooden, painted bird feeders. Three wooden picnic tables stood on one side of the building. Inside, Mimi and Ed were rushed off their feet with customers both local and out-of-towners browsing tables of stacked goods.

"Candles?" I mouthed to Ed as he helped a man buying a phone charger.

He motioned to the stockroom. I nipped behind the counter and went into the large room that held boxes of supplies. I lifted lids until Mimi appeared. She wore jeans and a sweatshirt that portrayed a trio of cat faces surrounded by flowers.

"Here, hun, Ed said you wanted candles. They're over this way."

I followed her and accepted a full box checking to make sure they were marked beeswax. "Thanks, Mimi, I hope we have plenty more. Nathaniel Playford wants some now."

She sniffed. "Probably for his personal use."

"Oh," I said in a leading tone. I wanted to hear from Mimi herself what she knew about Nathaniel Playford.

"Mimi!" Ed called.

"Sorry, I've got to go. We're wonderfully busy!" she said with a delighted grin.

I thanked her and started back down Main Street, thwarted and still fuming. What made Nathaniel think I was a spinster? Twenty-seven and unmarried today meant nothing. Had Flynn spoken to him yet? Should I try to talk to Nathaniel again? What could I say that I hadn't already to appeal to his better nature, that is, if he had one?

But as it turned out, I needn't have worried about what to say.

As I stepped into the Assembly Rooms, I saw Nathaniel Playford face-down on the floor, a dark red stain across the back of his fine, light-colored shirt.

Betsy Bell stood over him, a pair of bloody scissors in her hand.

Chapter Five

The box of candles slipped out of my arms and scattered onto the floor, the sound echoing in the deadly silent room. One candle rolled into the bottle of Hurdee Gurdee soda resting several inches from Nathaniel Playford's lifeless hand. A hysterical laugh threatened to burst from me as I thought that Nathaniel had been caught dead with a bottle of Hurdee Gurdee. Mercifully, I stopped myself, knowing it was shock.

Betsy Bell hadn't moved. She seemed frozen in place as blood dripped from the ornate scissors onto a very dead Nathaniel Playford.

"Betsy Bell, it's me, Kay. What happened here?"

She slowly turned toward me. Her eyes were opened wide in her chalk white face.

She moved her mouth, but no sound came out.

"Those are the scissors from your store, aren't they? The special ones that you have made up as gifts for good customers, right? Let's put them on the table here while we talk."

She nodded and almost in slow motion, moved to the table. She looked at the scissors with a kind of horror. They fell from her hand and clattered onto the table.

At that moment, Flynn came into the room at the far end from the door leading to the kitchens. He saw Betsy Bell drop the scissors and stood stock still at the scene before him.

Betsy Bell gasped at his sudden appearance, sharply sucking in her breath. Shaking, she fell into my arms. "I had to come back for my scissors," she whispered for my ears only.

Flynn stared at Nathaniel Playford's body, then looked from Betsy Bell to me. As our eyes met, I felt a chill. *He'd better not be thinking of that text I sent him. And how long had he been here? Had he seen the murderer? He surely didn't think Betsy Bell had killed Nathaniel.*

"It's all right," I told Betsy Bell, holding her upright and feeling that it certainly wasn't all right.

Flynn dropped down next to Nathaniel and checked for a pulse. He shook his head at me, then pulled out his cell phone and moved away.

I rubbed Betsy Bell's back. "You came back for your scissors."

She nodded her head. "I don't have many of them and they're expensive. I don't know if I can afford to have any more made."

Flynn finished his call and looked like he would speak. I gave him a sharp look. He stared at me, but remained by the body and said nothing.

"Betsy Bell, what were your scissors doing over here in...um, at the Assembly Rooms?"

"Miss Scales had torn her hem while she was dancing," she told me, still in that terrified whisper. "She texted me asking if I could come and fix it."

Miss Scales was the primary school's second-grade teacher. "And you did?"

Betsy Bell finally stepped back. Her voice regained a little of its strength. "Yes. I had made the gown for Miss Scales. It was only right that I repair the hem. I ran over and fixed it so she could continue her dancing lesson. Later, when I was at my store, I realized I'd forgotten my scissors and came back for them."

She started to turn and look at Nathaniel's body, but I gently turned her face back to me. "Where were the scissors?"

"In-in Nathaniel's back," she said.

I wanted to ask her why she'd pulled them out of the man's body, but the sound of sirens outside the building stopped me.

A man and a woman dressed in the county's medical response team's brown uniforms entered the room. They carried a duffel bag, black cases, and a collapsible stretcher. With them were Detective Derek Gordon and Officer Keona Fowler. Officer Fowler had been sent over from Harrisonburg to help during the festival. Another officer began putting up bright yellow crime scene tape.

Detective Gordon—I didn't think now would be a good time to call him Derek—pulled on gloves and walked briskly to the body. He was a tall, fit man with blond hair cut short.

Officer Fowler flipped open her notebook and began making notes. She was dark-skinned with short curly hair and wore a bright shade of pink lipstick. I'd bet old Sheriff Wilkinson wouldn't ap-

prove of the lipstick, but since he spent most of the winter travel-
ing to somewhere warm where he could go fishing, she only had
Detective Gordon to answer to.

The response team began taking photographs of the body. Detective Gordon and Officer Fowler came over and stood in front
of us, Flynn along with them.

"Okay, who's going to tell me what happened here?" the detective asked.

I thought fast. While I was certain Betsy Bell hadn't killed
Nathaniel, things didn't look good for her. She needed an attorney.

"Someone has stabbed Nathaniel Playford in the back," I said,
stating the obvious. "Betsy Bell left her scissors here earlier and
whoever stabbed him used her scissors."

"Were you the one who discovered the body, Miss Starling?"
Detective Gordon asked.

"Um, well, in a way—"

"No, Kay came in *after* I found my scissors," Betsy Bell interrupted in her normal soft, gentle voice.

"Betsy Bell, you don't have to say anything right now," I told her,
my voice firm. "You should have an attorney when you talk to the
police."

"But it's Derek, not some outsider." She proceeded to tell the
detective what she'd told me about how Miss Scales tore her hem
prompting her to come and fix it, then realizing she'd left her
scissors here and returning for them.

"So, are you saying that you came here, saw the murder weapon in the victim's back and removed it?" the detective asked, his head tilted to one side.

Betsy Bell nodded. "They are *my* scissors. What would people say?"

"I see. Have you been taking dancing lessons from Mr. Playford, Miss Ward?"

"No."

"Did you know him at all?"

"A little bit," she said. "He'd lost one of the buttons on his breeches. He brought them to my store so we could find a match."

"When was this?"

"Yesterday."

"And did you find a match?"

"We did. I have hundreds of buttons if not thousands," Betsy Bell looked around proudly. "I don't want people to have to leave our town to get buttons so I keep a big supply. Even Nathaniel said he'd never seen so many buttons."

Officer Fowler looked up from her notes to shoot a look of disbelief at Detective Gordon.

He stripped off his gloves, jammed them in his pocket, and continued the questioning. "You talked with Nathaniel Playford while matching the button?"

Betsy Bell nodded. "He was very complimentary of my store. He came in at lunchtime and ended up taking me to the Golden Age Diner for a grilled cheese sandwich as a way of thanking me for my help. I told him he didn't need to but he insisted." She avoided the detective's eyes.

Officer Fowler handed Detective Gordon a bag marked "Evidence" containing the scissors. The scissors had "Happy Fabrics" engraved on the ornate handle.

"May I have those back when you're done with them?" Betsy Bell asked.

Detective Gordon ran a hand over his face.

Then he turned his attention to Flynn. "When did you get here and what did you see, Mr. Holden?"

"I received a text from Kay regarding Nathaniel so I popped in to have a word with him. I came in through the kitchen entrance. Kay was here with Betsy Bell standing by the table when I walked into the room. Nathaniel was on the floor, not moving. I checked for a pulse but found none."

"Were the scissors still in Mr. Playford's back when you came in?"

"Er, no," Flynn said.

"Where were they?"

The normally cool and confident Flynn Holden looked uncomfortable.

"Mr. Holden?" Detective Gordon prodded. "You own this building, don't you?"

"Yes."

"Where were the scissors when you entered this room?"

"In Betsy Bell's right hand."

"Did you see anyone coming out of this room when you arrived?"

"No."

"What was the text about?" the detective asked, circling back.

Flynn hesitated, then said, "Kay had been concerned about Nathaniel's attitude and behavior towards women during his dancing classes."

"What about his behavior?" Detective Gordon asked.

"He was a flirt," Flynn said.

"It was more than flirting," I corrected. "He was crude and disrespectful. I thought he might cause a scandal and effect the festival and thus the town's future," I said.

"Were you concerned, Mr. Holden?"

"Somewhat. I've known—I knew Nathaniel for about a year. I wasn't aware of him causing trouble, but that doesn't mean he didn't."

Detective Gordon looked at Flynn. "Let me see the text you received from Miss Starling."

My chest went tight.

"Is that necessary?" Flynn asked, one eyebrow raised. "I've told you what it was about."

"Yes, it is, unless you want to be charged with obstruction in a murder investigation," Detective Gordon said.

Reluctantly, Flynn handed him his phone.

"Vile, loathsome man! I could kill him," Detective Gordon read aloud, then looked at me.

"I didn't kill him," I said. "It's something people say when they're frustrated and angry."

"I didn't accuse you of murder, Miss Starling," he said.

"She's telling the truth," Flynn said in the tense silence that followed. "When I came in, it was Betsy Bell that was holding the scissors. She dropped them on to the table there."

"Is that correct, Miss Ward?"

Betsy Bell nodded.

We all turned as the medical team wheeled Nathaniel Playford's body, now inside a body bag, outside.

Detective Gordon said, "Betsy Bell Ward, I'd like you to come along to the police station with me for further questioning regarding the murder of Nathaniel Playford. Kay Starling, Flynn Holden, I'll need the two of you as well."

My phone chimed. "It's Hayley," I said to Detective Gordon. "She and the other members of the planning committee will need to know where I am. We have a meeting scheduled for this evening. The festival starts tomorrow. May I answer her?"

"You can text her. Make it brief."

"Where are you? "Hayley asked.

"At the corner of Despair and Hades."

"I heard sirens! My anxiety is on high."

"There's been an incident at the Assembly Rooms. I'll be at the police station."

"What! I'm on my way."

"Maybe that's not a good idea."

I stared at my phone, but she didn't answer back.

As we were herded into patrol cars, fear rose in me. A man was dead, yes, but what would happen to the festival? To the community? To all the people who believed in Jane Austen Town? Would our plans fail because people didn't want to come to a small town where there'd just been a murder? What would Aunt Adeline think?

I'd been afraid that Nathaniel Playford might cause a scandal with his despicable ways with women. I never thought the scandal would be his murder. What would happen to Betsy Bell? No way she had killed him. But who had?

My fingers reached for my Jane Austen pendant. I couldn't count on Detective Gordon to find the culprit. He was a good man, but I saw the calculating way he'd looked at Betsy Bell. I also knew he considered me a suspect after Flynn showed him my text.

I would have to dig around, find out who was angry at, possibly hated Nathaniel Playford, and discover the identity of the murderer myself.

Chapter Six

"I 'm telling all y'all, the festival is doomed!" Mayor Walter "Buster" Buckalew IV exclaimed. "Are you sure we should go ahead with it, Adeline?"

It was almost nine o'clock that night. We sat around the farmhouse kitchen table back at Starling Farm; myself, Hugo, Hayley, Flynn, and Guthrie who sat next to Aunt Adeline with his hand on the back of her chair and was the recipient of jealous looks from the mayor.

After we'd been released from questioning at the police station, Betsy Bell declined the offer to have someone stay with her, saying she only wanted sleep. She needed to get up very early to set up her sales tent. Since her interview with Detective Gordon, she had seemed withdrawn. We'd seen her home safely, then come back to Starling Farm.

Aunt Adeline had forbidden us to talk about the murder until we'd finished eating her delicious, homemade chicken and dumplings. I didn't think I'd have an appetite, but at the first whiff, I remembered I hadn't eaten since breakfast and tucked in.

Ida Calhoun, Aunt Adeline's part-time housekeeper whom she'd known since they were teenagers, had stayed late and was clearing the table.

"Buster, you haven't got a lick of sense," Aunt Adeline said, handing her clean plate to Mrs. Calhoun with a smile. "The festival starts in a matter of hours."

Mayor Buckalew paced. "As soon as people hear about the vicious slaying of the dancing fellow, they'll cancel their plans to come here. We'll have to refund their tickets. How will we do that when we've already spent most of the money? Coralie thinks we should call Silas Dale and take him up on the casino offer before he withdraws it."

"That's a terrible idea and against what the town wants," Guthrie said.

"The town manager is wrong," Aunt Adeline said. "No one has cancelled, have they, Hayley?"

Hayley pulled her iPad from her bag under the table and tapped quickly. "No, ma'am. No requests on the website's email. We've actually sold more tickets than we'd hoped for."

"You see, Buster? Now take a deep breath and let's see how things play out," Aunt Adeline said. "Are you sure you don't want some chicken and dumplings?"

The mayor shook his head. "I couldn't swallow a bite. But speaking of food, did I tell you that Silas Dale promised to put Buster's Big Size Pies in vending machines all over the casino resort?"

Only every time we've seen you since Silas Dale's offer.

His phone rang before Aunt Adeline could read him the lecture I saw brewing on her face. He took the call. "No, I hadn't thought of that. Maybe? I suppose not. I'll ask Ad—the planning committee."

He ended the call. "Do you think we should cancel the archery practice in Dogwood Park on Saturday? Seeing as how the dancing fellow was stabbed to death, Coralie thinks archery would be in bad taste."

"Mayor," I said. "We're about to discuss any changes to the festival now. We'll consider the issue. Perhaps you'll excuse us."

"Yes, good night, Buster," Aunt Adeline said.

Looking hangdog, the mayor walked out the back door.

"Good riddance," Guthrie muttered.

Aunt Adeline let out a breath. "That man would give an aspirin a headache."

"Woof!" Bowie agreed. Hugo bent to pet his dog.

Ida Calhoun put out a coconut cake she'd made and began passing slices around.

"No, thank you," Flynn told her when she offered him a plate.

Hayley snorted. I realized that she'd turned chilly toward Flynn since she found out he'd shown Detective Gordon that ill-conceived text I'd sent saying I could kill Nathaniel.

"How is Sharon, Mrs. Calhoun?" I asked, hoping she wasn't offended by Flynn's refusal of her cake.

"She's not happy about losing her job with Miss Josie, of course. She's still living with me in my trailer. She's picked up a part-time job in online customer service. At least it's for a yarn company. Sharon loves to knit."

"Sharon will be helping me at the bakery tent during the festival. I'll be grateful for another pair of hands," Hayley said. She put down her fork. "This is one excellent cake, Mrs. Calhoun. I have to pace myself so I don't eat my slice in under a minute. I've got more sense than to ask you for the recipe, but it sure is good."

Ida smiled and brushed down her blue apron. "Thank you, Miss Hayley. You're a fine baker yourself." She moved back toward the sink, humming softly under her breath.

"That she is," Guthrie said, smiling at Hayley.

"All right," Aunt Adeline said. "I want to hear everything that happened today. I'm as sorry as I can be that I had to run out of town today of all days, but it couldn't be helped."

"Are you going to tell us where you went, Aunt Adeline?" Hugo asked.

She nodded. "Briefly as we've got important matters to discuss, although not the archery lessons. They stay. Anyway, Kay and Hugo might remember me mentioning my friend Olive Howard over the years. She lives up north of Elkton, almost to Luray. She's reclusive, so we don't see one another often."

"Oh yes," I said. "She shares your love of Siamese cats." I froze for a second hoping I hadn't just brought back the pain of Aunt Adeline losing her last Siamese, Rama, at Easter.

Aunt Adeline paused, then said, "That's right, Kay. We met way back in the seventies on a train coming down from Washington. She had a Siamese cat in a carrier. I was only fifteen years old at the time, and Olive was almost thirty. We ended up having quite an adventure when the train got stuck on the tracks, but I'm digressing. Around two o'clock, I received an urgent call from the woman caring for Olive. Olive is eighty and not as spry as Miss June at the diner. She's been living on her own until now. Apparently, she thought she could sneak her Siamese cat, Cho, into the assisted living facility with her. Of course, they won't allow it. Olive was distraught to say the least and dug in her heels saying that if she had to give him up, I was the only person she'd give him to."

"How awful to be parted from a pet that way," Flynn said.

Since when do you like pets? You don't have a dog or cat or even a goldfish that I know of.

"Guthrie drove me up there and it was so sad, Flynn. Olive cried her heart out. I told her that Cho would have a wonderful place to live and that I'd bring him back for a visit maybe next April. I want him to get settled in with me first. She seemed easier in her mind then and proceeded to tell me all about him and give me copious instructions about his care."

"Cho is here now?" I asked.

"Yes," Aunt Adeline said. "I have him set up in my suite upstairs and will ease him into the rest of the house after the festival. Hugo, don't take Bowie upstairs for the time being."

"Yes, ma'am," Hugo agreed.

"Then when Guthrie brought me home, I knew that someone had died."

"Indeed, you did, Addie," Guthrie said.

We all looked at Aunt Adeline, waiting for her to elaborate.

"Well, the white stag was out in the field past the stables," Aunt Adeline said as if that explained everything.

I kept my eyes on her, resisting the urge to look at Hayley. Neither of us believed in this mysterious white stag who was a harbinger of death. If I looked at Hayley, there was sure to be mutual eye-rolling, which would be disrespectful.

Hugo averted his face and bent to give Bowie a bite of cake. He didn't think much of the white stag theory either.

Flynn's eyebrows drew together. "I didn't realize there were white stags here in the States. In Britain, they're rare and considered to be from the Otherworld. They've been known to bring messages."

At his words, I was certain that an entire amusement park of expressions crossed my face. I put my hand up and rubbed my forehead. I couldn't have been more surprised than if he told me he had video of the Loch Ness Monster.

"Precisely, Flynn." Aunt Adeline sat back in her chair. "Now, let me hear what's happened."

I described first my meeting with Nathaniel Playford, getting the candles from Monday's Country Store, then finding Betsy Bell standing over Nathaniel's dead body, and Detective Gordon and Officer Fowler questioning us. When I got to the part about Flynn showing Detective Gordon my text, Flynn said, "Detective Gordon threatened to charge me with obstruction if I refused to give him my phone."

"Probably would have been better if you deleted the text after you read it in the first place, don't you think, Flynn?" Hayley asked in a tone that suggested Flynn was five years old.

"Sorry," he said. "I didn't think to do so."

"It was unfortunate," Aunt Adeline said. "But Guthrie and I know from watching *Midsomer Murders* that they can retrieve deleted texts nowadays."

"Nothing good ever comes from technology," Guthrie grumbled.

"At the police station, Detective Gordon questioned me again, then I had to make a formal statement," I said.

Flynn nodded. "That's what I experienced. I expect when the detective finished with Kay, he started with me."

"You waited with only a cold cup of tea, isn't that what you told me?" I couldn't resist mentioning.

"And some peanut butter crackers, yes," Flynn said gravely.

How did he rate peanut butter crackers?

Hayley leaned forward. "I don't know what is going on in Derek Gordon's head. How on God's green earth he could think that Betsy Bell Ward could possibly stab someone—with her own scissors no less—is beyond me. Kay and Flynn are suspects too. I flat out told Derek he was crazy and ridiculous."

I'd heard them yelling at one another. There'd be no coming back from some of the words Hayley'd used to describe her disappointment in Detective Gordon.

"Lost your boyfriend, eh, Hailstorm," Hugo said.

Hayley's hair swung in a puffy arc as she whipped around to face Hugo. "He is not my boyfriend!"

"That's what I said."

Hayley flicked her fingers at him. "Don't talk to me."

Aunt Adeline crossed her arms. "What I find extraordinary is that you, Kay, and you, Flynn, went down to the police station and willingly gave statements to law enforcement without an attorney present! Not only you two, but timid little Betsy Bell! What were you thinking? I'd say you believed it was just Derek, didn't you? No harm could come from talking to Derek."

"Yes, ma'am, although the thought did cross my mind that Betsy Bell should have an attorney," I said, running my finger against the grain of the white tablecloth that had snowmen marching around the border.

"It was unwise, Mrs. Starling, you're right," Flynn said. "I think I can speak for myself, Kay, and Betsy Bell when I say we were all in shock."

"You may call me Adeline, Flynn. I'll telephone Brock Winthrop before it gets much later. He's the best criminal attorney in central Virginia. Kay, who do you think killed this dancing master?"

"I honestly don't know. We need to question people, find out what Nathaniel has been doing since he arrived in Jane Austen Town. More importantly who he's been seeing, who was angry with him. Alexandra Bartholomew, the woman who runs a B & B in Massachusetts, was angry with him the first time I was at the Assembly Rooms. She gave him some choice words in a heated whisper and he laughed in her face. Wait, I just realized something," I said, sitting up straighter. "When I came back with the candles, I could smell her perfume when I first walked in the door."

"Are you sure?" Flynn asked.

"Yes. It's J'adore by Dior."

"I know that one," Aunt Adeline said. "Been around for ages and easily recognizable."

"I was gone about twenty-five minutes. Alexandra could have come in, seen the scissors, stabbed Nathaniel, and left in that time," I said.

"Why would she do that?" Hugo asked.

"I'll have to question her," I said, "But if I had to make a guess, Nathaniel was involved with her romantically and they quarreled. And another thing. Flynn, do you know if Playford was really Nathaniel's last name?"

"On it," Hayley said, tapping on her iPad.

Ida Calhoun dropped a dish in the sink.

"I'd never thought about it," Flynn said. "There's been no reason to question his identity. I can ring one of my colleagues and see if she knows anything. What makes you suspect he was using an alias?"

"It's just a hunch. In the late 1600s to early 1700s, a man named John Playford published multiple editions of a dancing manual for English country dances." I searched my brain. "*The Dancing Master*, that's what it was called. Nathaniel could have taken the name professionally."

Flynn rubbed his chin, calling my attention to his sexy five-o'clock shadow. "Clearly, Detective Gordon will know

Nathaniel's real name. Whether or not he'll share that information with us is doubtful, I'd think."

"I agree," Aunt Adeline said. "We can't count on Derek to be open with information."

"Derek may not, but I will," Hayley said triumphantly. "His name was Grant, Nathaniel Grant. It's right here in one of his earlier YouTube videos."

I dashed around the table to see what she was looking at. "This is from eleven years ago."

Hayley turned the volume up and we all heard Nathaniel's voice introducing himself as Nathaniel Grant. I felt a shiver go down my spine hearing the dead man's voice.

Flynn stood behind Hayley. "That must be when he first created his channel. He published dancing manuals. He said the YouTube videos helped him with sales and with securing jobs at various events."

"Later, seven years ago," Hayley said, moving her fingers across the keypad, "He made an announcement on his channel that he'd henceforth be known as Nathaniel Playford after the great dancing master of the 17th century."

"Well remembered, Kay," Flynn said with an approving glance at me.

Praise from Flynn. Was it too late in the day to buy a lottery ticket?

"I've always said that your English history obsession comes in handy sometimes, sis," Hugo teased.

I felt heat rise to my face at the compliments, but my eyes stayed on Nathaniel's YouTube channel. "Good work, Hayley. Go back to his first video from eleven years ago please."

Once again, we heard Nathaniel's voice and watched him introduce himself. He was thinner, but his hair was the same as was that air of smugness about him. He stood against a fake background of dancers in costumes at a Regency ball. "And remember, as Jane Austen said, 'to be fond of dancing was a certain step towards falling in love.'" He snickered, then, "You will receive excellent instruction from me if you sign up for one of my classes or purchase one of my manuals. You'll learn steps, gain confidence, and prepare to have fun at your next English country dance. No experience necessary!"

He ended this speech by bowing with a flourish.

"Stop! Stop the video right there, Hayley," I said.

"Here?" she asked.

"Back it up to when he begins the bow. That's it. Look at his left hand," I said.

Hugo whistled. "He's wearing a wedding ring. He sure didn't act married that night we were at Gator's."

"He never said a word to me about being married or having an ex-wife," Flynn said, his voice full of surprise.

Ida Calhoun said a soft goodnight and went out the back door.

"Who was he married to? Someone in Williamsburg?" Aunt Adeline asked.

"Not only *who* was she, but *where* is she now? Is there animosity between them?" I asked. "Marriage records don't become public record in Virginia until after twenty-five years. How are we going to find out who she is?"

"He worked up and down the east coast. She could be anywhere. We better find her," Hayley said. "Because maybe she killed him."

Chapter Seven

T he first day of the festival, Friday morning, December 12, dawned bright and sunny, promising to be in the upper fifties to low sixties. I'd abandoned my morning run for the duration of the festival. I dressed in a sky-blue Regency gown and blue, ballet-like flats. My gold Jane Austen silhouette pendant was around my neck giving me an extra boost of confidence. Since the Promenade would be this afternoon featuring Miss Austen's Militia, I buttoned a royal blue spencer jacket in a military style over my dress. I drew out a newly-purchased Regency shako hat in a matching royal blue with sky-blue trim and a cockade with a fake white feather. I settled it on my head.

Aunt Adeline had invited me to have a light breakfast in her suite. Glancing at my phone, I saw I had enough time to feed my outdoor friends. Now that it was cooler, I made sure to give them plenty of peanuts and bird seed. I stepped into the brick folly and grabbed a gallon of water. I had just filled all three bird baths when a movement in one of Aunt Adeline's windows caught my eye.

I smiled when I realized Cho had been watching me and tapping his tail on the window.

Finishing up, I saw Henry Tilney, the crow, and some of his friends fly overhead, waiting for me to leave so they could have breakfast. "Tilney, you'd better behave, you hear me! I don't want to see you cruising past the windows, teasing Cho. Don't make me put you on rations."

"Caw! Caw!" Tilney, I knew it was him, called, then swooped down and plucked the feather from my new hat. He flew away with it. My hat fell from my head to the ground.

"Naughty bird!" I yelled at him as he soared overhead, hardly able to believe his audacity. I picked up my shako, brushed it off, and jammed it back on my head.

I stomped all the way back to the house in a most unladylike manner.

Inside, I climbed up the stairs to Aunt Adeline's suite. This consisted of her bedroom, a spacious bathroom, and a prettily decorated room she called her sitting room.

"Good morning, Kay," Aunt Adeline said while looking over my outfit. "You need to pin up your hair and leave some curls to peek out of that darling hat. Meanwhile, come and have a bite to eat."

Her own ensemble consisted of a long-sleeved, bronze-colored Regency gown with a golden stripe running through it. A snug, golden velvet turban with a rhinestone brooch covered all but a few curls on her head.

"My hat was even prettier until Tilney, the crow, flew at my head and stole my feather."

Aunt Adeline chuckled. "Showing you some affection."

I sat down in one of the comfortable chairs, smoothing the back of my gown as I did so.

The sitting room was decorated in pinks and burgundy. Between two burgundy Queen Anne chairs, a circular, antique table contained a white, thermal coffee carafe, white mugs, a plate of blueberry muffins and, under a kitchen towel to keep them warm, egg and sausage muffins.

"I was outside and thought I saw Cho in the window," I said as Aunt Adeline poured me a cup of coffee.

"He's doing surprisingly well," she said. "Slept in bed with me all night. Oh, here he is."

Cho walked into the room with all the elegance his breed is known for. His long, fawn-colored body was sleek and muscular. His elegant legs ended in dark brown paws which matched his tail, his ears, and his face. His whiskers were long and white.

I gasped when he moved close enough for me to really see him. "His eyes are amazing. Almost unreal. I've never seen that shade of sapphire blue on a cat before, even in photos," I said. "Look, they shift from sapphire blue to a shade of purple."

Aunt Adeline fidgeted in her chair. "Yes, I know. His eyes are unique, yet, when I first met Olive all those years ago, I could swear she had a cat with the same color eyes."

We both stared at the cat who'd moved toward the pink floral sofa. He effortlessly jumped to the cushion, turned around four times, and lay like a cat-model. Or a king.

"Two cats with those exceptional eyes?" I asked reaching for a blueberry muffin.

Aunt Adeline hesitated, then said, "Perhaps Olive went to the same breeder."

For fifty years? No way. There was something about Cho Aunt Adeline wasn't telling me.

"Now Kay, there are a few last-minute things to discuss before the festival starts at ten o' clock. As Hayley said last night, ticket sales have been gratifyingly brisk. We'll want to keep talk of Nathaniel's demise to the bare minimum. I spoke to Neil last night. He wasn't best pleased, but he agreed to write in the *Jane Austen Town Gazette* that Nathaniel had 'died suddenly' and that 'police are investigating' rather than use the word murder."

I brushed my fingers on a napkin. "That's good news, but I don't know how long we can keep the murder quiet." A movement from the sofa caught my eye. Cho seemed to be listening with interest to our conversation.

"It seems mercenary and maybe it is, but we have to try for the town's sake," Aunt Adeline said. "We want people to come to the festival and stay. Shouting from the rooftops that the dancing master has been stabbed to death won't bring him back anyway."

"True."

"I will be teaching the dancing classes now. I know all the English country dances from my involvement with the Jane Austen Guild of America."

"Are you sure? I know you want to go around the festival and talk to people and you're hosting a card party tomorrow night. You're not doing too much, are you?" As soon as the words were out of my mouth, I regretted them.

"I'm quite capable," Aunt Adeline said with energy. "And since you will be spending your time investigating the murder, someone else will teach the Regency Games class."

"Yes, ma'am."

"Speaking of the murder, Betsy Bell is a sweet girl but she was on the scene before anyone else. Nathaniel was killed with a pair of her scissors. I spoke to Brock Winthrop last night. He's driving over from Charlottesville this afternoon as a special favor to me. I want you to tell Betsy Bell the attorney is here to help her. I know she has a display and sales tent set up for today, but she needs someone to cover for her when Brock gets here so she can meet with him."

I tapped notes on my phone. "I'll take care of it. Text me when Mr. Winthrop is here. While I'm watching over the festival, I want to squeeze in some time to go to the Golden Age diner. Maybe Francie will remember something useful about Betsy Bell's lunch with Nathaniel. I need to speak with Alexandra too."

"When did Flynn get to the Assembly Rooms?"

I drew back. "Flynn? Do you suspect him?'

"I like him, and he comes from a good family, but I don't know him well. I'm angry that he even mentioned that text you sent him, no less showed it to Detective Gordon."

"It bothers me too." *Too much.* "As for when he got to the Assembly Rooms, I really don't know. He came into the ballroom from the kitchens."

"So, it's *possible* that he went there to talk to Nathaniel as he told you he would in his text, they argued, and Flynn stabbed him."

"If you go with the conventional wisdom that anyone is capable of committing murder, then yes it's possible," I said, feeling the blueberry muffin turning over in my stomach.

"We must go by that wisdom," Aunt Adeline said, looking at me intently. "We must consider Betsy Bell, Flynn, Alexandra, and Nathaniel's unknown wife suspects until we rule them out."

"I suppose so, but I don't like it. Surely the killer is someone from outside of Jane Austen Town," I said.

"I hope so."

"I'm determined to find out who did it so that his murder does not affect the success of the festival. What will happen to everyone if that horrible Silas Dale brings his casino here?"

"That's commendable, but there's something you're not considering. Nathaniel's murderer must be identified because you, Kay, *are the only one who threatened to kill him.* You were alone with Betsy Bell when the body was found. A case could be made that the two of you planned his murder."

"Meow!" Cho agreed.

I glanced at him, then back to Aunt Adeline. "But that's absurd! I'd never kill anyone. You must know that!"

"I do. Does Detective Gordon? He'll have a great deal of pressure on him to arrest someone. Kay, what made you say such a thing in the first place?"

I shook my head. "Nathaniel Grant was a despicable man. If you *saw* the way he treated the ladies at the dancing class! His lewd comments and suggestive remarks were repulsive. I told you the way he spoke to me, and who knows what remark he made about

Hayley's fruit tarts." I threw up my hands. "I was frustrated. I had no idea someone would actually kill him a few minutes later."

She reached over and patted my knee. "All right. I only want to protect you, Kay. Will you be present when Brock interviews Betsy Bell?"

"If you think it necessary."

She smiled. "I do. Very well, let's go out and welcome people to our town. Today's our big day! I'm going to help Guthrie at his shop while he moves books to his sales tent, then I'm having lunch with one of our speakers. She's down from Ohio and giving a talk tonight in the church hall on Austen's life and work."

Aunt Adeline rose and walked into her bedroom.

I stayed behind a moment to pet Cho. He allowed me to rub and scratch gently around his ears. His fur was incredibly soft and his low purr made me smile. "I'm happy you're here, Cho. Aunt Adeline and I have missed Rama since he went to the Rainbow Bridge. I hope you'll like living with us. I wish I had more time to spend with you but with the festival, and now this murder," I trailed off.

He permitted me to stroke him for a few more minutes before tunneling under the pink and cream pillows piled on the end of the sofa until only the tip of his tail was visible.

I chuckled and went to my bathroom to work on my hair. The curling iron and I have never had the best of relationships, but after about twenty minutes, I was satisfied with the results.

Putting my hat back on so my new curls showed to advantage, and smoothing on a pair of white gloves, I ran down the stairs and flung open the front door.

Standing there about to knock was Flynn, dressed in scarlet regimentals, exactly like the ones George Wickham, the villain in *Pride and Prejudice,* had worn.

Chapter Eight

"Good morning, Kay. I see we're both dressed with Miss Austen's Militia in mind."

"Yes," I said, unable to shake Aunt Adeline's suspicions about him from my thoughts.

"See here, may I park my Lexus in your motor court during the festival? I hope it's agreeable. Main Street was closing to traffic as I pulled up."

I glanced over to where a newer model Lexus was parked next to my old Toyota. "Sure, no problem." I closed the door behind me.

As we walked down the long driveway, I asked him how the house his uncle had left him was coming along.

"Actually, I've not done much with it other than cleaning and painting. I've got to concentrate right now on making sure the vineyard is pruned and covered in mulch. I've left it a bit late. I was able to hire men who'd been laid off from the bottling plant to help. Luckily, we've only had the one hard freeze thus far."

"Do you plan to stay in the house once it's remodeled?"

"Like Starling Farm, it's an historic house, so it's more of a restoration than a remodel," he corrected.

Okay, okay, I couldn't be irritated at him for correcting me since I'd challenged him regarding historical accuracy so many times. But why didn't he answer my question about whether he intended to stay in town?

"I rang an old colleague of mine, Madison Miller Montgomery, at Colonial Williamsburg this morning regarding Nathaniel," he said, slowing his pace. "She works in public relations."

"What did you find out?"

"Not much. It was a bit uncomfortable speaking to her. She and Nathaniel used to see one another—"

"They were dating?" I interrupted.

"Er, yes, a year ago. I chiefly wanted to break the news of his death to her rather than have her read it online."

"I see. Was she very upset?"

He cleared his throat. "Not especially. But before you think that she might be a suspect, she isn't."

"How do you know that?"

"Because their relationship was long over, and she bore him no ill will. In fact, she's engaged to a cardiologist now."

I'd trade the dancing master for a cardiologist, too.

"Okay."

"I managed to ask her if she knew about Nathaniel being married at some point. She was totally in the dark about it. Said Nathaniel had never mentioned an ex-wife."

"It seems like he wanted to keep his ex-wife a secret. Divorce is all too common, so it's not that he's ashamed of having a failed marriage. Maybe it's that he's ashamed of *her*," I said.

"Possibly. At any rate, Maddy promised to discreetly ask around and see if anyone else knew about Nathaniel's marriage."

Maddy?

"Um, good," I said.

"Hey y'all, come help me carry these tubs!" Hayley called as we reached the end of the driveway.

She had on a pretty, but simple, Regency gown of light green that matched her eyes and complemented her light brown skin. Pearls encircled her neck and adorned her ears. Her wild mane of curls had been pulled up into a topknot and she had green silk flowers pinned around it.

"Good morning, my lady," I said, bobbing a curtsy.

She tried to curtsy, but couldn't with the weight of the tubs in her hands. "Hi, Kay. Help!"

Flynn hurried toward her and took both tubs of food off her hands. "Allow me."

She smiled politely at him in a way that told me he was not out of the woods as far as she was concerned. Still, I had the strangest feeling. Almost like jealousy. But it couldn't be that. I could never be interested in him. Flynn was too serious. Flynn was a strictly by the rule book man. Flynn didn't like sugary treats.

A loud laugh caught our attention. "Hailstorm, your hair done up that way makes you at least four inches taller. But you'll never be as tall as me," Hugo said gesturing to his top hat.

He was dressed as a Regency coachman in boots, breeches, and a shirt and cravat all topped with a heavy black greatcoat with three capes at the shoulder. He looked quite dashing. The carriage rides in Dogwood Park were sure to be a success.

Her hands free now, Hayley patted her big hair like the little red-haired girl in the comic strip *Peanuts*. "You're just jealous. Don't think I haven't noticed that bald spot coming up on the back of your head."

"A little thinning does not constitute baldness," he snapped.

Hayley bit her lip and shot me a look that said she knew she'd gone too far.

"Hugo," I cautioned.

He bowed. "Beg pardon, Miss Hailstorm. I'm naturally flattered that you've paid such close attention to my appearance."

At that moment, a man dressed in a similar outfit to Hugo's strode up with Bowie.

"Oh no you didn't, Hugo," Hayley said.

But he had. I laughed in delight. Hugo had given Bowie a small top hat to match his own. It was kept in place with a blue ribbon tied under the dog's chin.

Flynn balanced the food tubs and kneeled down so he could pet the dog.

Hugo gestured to the man and said, "This is my buddy, Percy Ryland. He's driving the other carriage."

Percy, a lean, athletic man with an earnest smile, whipped off his felt hat and bowed. "Nice to meet y'all," he said, his eyes on Hayley.

Hugo scowled.

Since Hugo wasn't doing it, I introduced everyone then asked, "Where are you from, Percy?"

"I have a horse farm south of Charlottesville near Esmont, a town of four hundred ninety-one persons," he said.

"Is that right," Hayley said with approval. "I wonder, Percy, if you could help me with some supplies for my tent, Hayley's Bakery?"

"Be my pleasure," Percy said happily.

The two walked away.

Hugo called Bowie to his side. "That's nice to see. Hayley could do worse than Percy Ryland, that's for sure. Percy and I are talking about going into business together, so he'll be here in town often."

"She just met the man and you're marrying her off?" I asked, puzzled.

"Why not? We *are* in Jane Austen Town where every story ends happily. I have to get going over to Dogwood Park. See you, Sis, Flynn," he said and walked down the street.

My gaze followed him, and suddenly I took in the whole of Main Street. I gasped.

"I know you were worried, Kay, but look at the crowds coming in," Flynn said.

He was right. The festival had only opened a few minutes ago and people were pouring in, each wearing a white wristband made of ribbon bearing the words "Celebrating 250 Years of Jane Austen" in gold letters. Many were in Regency costume. Some ladies held parasols. They wove their way through the far end of the white tents, gowns fluttering, and looked in shop windows.

I let out a big breath of relief and then drew in the scent of pine and woodsmoke. Eric Longo and Tyler Carter, our fire chief, were raising the huge Christmas tree onto the platform on the village green. Tyler had positioned a ladder, and several townspeople were standing by with boxes of Christmas tree decorations. Someone else set up music and strains of a Haydn piece met my ears.

"Haydn's London Symphonies. An excellent choice," Flynn remarked. "Let's take these tubs to Hayley's tent."

"I was about to suggest that," I said, turning my steps in the direction of Hayley's tent. "After we stop at Hayley's, I want to check out Guthrie's tent before I make my way to the Golden Age diner to question Francie."

"We are both going to the Golden Age diner to question Francie."

"I'd be delighted to have your company," I said insincerely.

It was easy to find Hayley's Bakery tent as Hayley had chosen to distinguish it with bright pink fabric curtains on three sides. A sign outside read "Hayley's Bakery," and a wooden sandwich board sign described the special "Tea Plate," featuring finger sandwiches, a scone, a slice of cake, and a Jane Austen silhouette cookie along with a cup of tea. Six, white, plastic tables for two outside the tent invited people to sit and eat. Inside, long folding tables had been set up as a workspace.

Sharon Calhoun stood inside pouring tea from a tea urn into cups for an older couple dressed in costume.

Valeria, Dessert Decorator Extraordinaire, looked up as we entered the tent. She grinned at Flynn. "Hey, a handsome man in uniform just in time with those tubs of goodies." She took the tubs from Flynn and put them down. She reached inside and pulled out a box of the Jane Austen silhouette cookies and started to place them on paper plates, offering one to Flynn. He shook his head no. She gave one to me. "How are you, Kay?"

"I'm good. I see it's blue winged eyeliner today, Valeria. Matches your gingham dress." I took a bite of my cookie.

She took a step closer to me and spoke in a low voice. "I considered wearing black as a mark of respect for the murdered man, but since I didn't know him, and I hear bad things about him, I went with my blue."

"Good choice. I'll bet you're the one who designed and made these delicious Austen cookies."

"What can I say? I love Jane. Speaking of love," she looked pointedly at Flynn, who was unloading the tubs, and back to me. "I see you together a lot."

"We're working on the festival, that's all. He doesn't even like me, Valeria, and sometimes the feeling is mutual."

She shook her head. "What a waste. If I didn't have my Antonio, I would bake that British hunk fresh scones every day."

Hayley and Percy appeared, Hayley giggling at something Percy said. They put on pink nitrile gloves, then went inside the tent and started arranging the contents of the "Tea Plate" on disposable plates.

"These egg salad sandwich fingers are my Granny's recipe, just so y'all know," Hayley informed us.

"Made with Duke's mayonnaise?" Percy asked.

"Is there another kind of mayo? Cause if there is, I don't know about it," Hayley quipped.

She and Percy laughed and added the food to each of the plates on the tables.

I walked out of the tent and moved down to where Sharon stood piling napkins in easy reach of customers. "Hey there, Sharon, how's it going?"

Sharon Calhoun was in her early forties, with shoulder length platinum blonde hair and an orangey shade of red lipstick. Not in costume, she wore jeans, a leopard-print sweater, and a blue windbreaker. A knitted headband held her hair back. "As usual, I'm working," she said, without a smile. "Thanks for asking."

I'd noticed that Sharon rarely smiled and put it down to her having a tough time raising her son alone and living with her mother in their trailer. She tended to be quiet. Josie had said Sharon was very efficient at her job at the bottling plant before it closed. "Has Palmer started back to school?"

She nodded. "He's a good young man. Going to be a great doctor one day. Can I get y'all anything?"

People were starting to line up behind us. I started to say no, but Flynn asked what kind of tea they were serving.

Sharon turned to the tea urns. "We have hot tea and iced tea."

For a split second, I caught Flynn's lips purse no doubt at the very idea of tea being served cold. Being English, he would consider serving tea cold an abomination.

"May I have a cup of hot tea, please?" he said, pulling out his debit card.

"It's on the house. Do you want sugar in it? Lemon?"

"No sugar. I'll have lemon and some milk, if you have it," he said and smiled at her.

She didn't return the smile but fixed his tea as he'd ordered. Handing it to him, she turned to me. "I heard about what happened to the dancing master." Like Valeria, she kept her voice low so customers wouldn't overhear. I thought it shook slightly. "Do they know who did it?"

I shook my head. "Not yet."

She nodded a little too fast and moved away to help a customer.

"A trifle nervous, wasn't she?" Flynn said as we turned our steps to find Guthrie's tent. "Do you think she knew Nathaniel?"

"It's possible of course, but I doubt it with her spending her days working first at the plant and then from home. She's upset like everyone else. Murder isn't common here."

Lorraine Longo, clipboard in hand, walked toward us.

"Good morning," I said. "How are you, Lorraine?"

She sighed. "Busy! And glad to be in this Regency dress. I didn't realize how comfortable it would be at eight months pregnant."

"You look great in it," I said.

"Can you point us in the direction of Guthrie's tent?" Flynn asked.

"In the next row, four tents up."

We thanked her and meandered past a tent with Jane Austen mugs, t-shirts, magnets, scarves, canvas totes, and other Janeite favorites, another tent featuring Regency shawls, and a third tent set up by the local hair salon demonstrating Regency hairstyles

and taking appointments for festival goers who wanted their own
Regency coiffure.

Guthrie's Books had a quote from Jane Austen's *Pride and
Prejudice* on an easel that read, "I declare after all there is no en-
joyment like reading." Various editions of all of Austen's books
including her *Juvenilia* were available for purchase. There was
also a small sign that read, "Ask about collectible editions." Once
again, I thought of Aunt Adeline's early edition copy of *Sense and
Sensibility* which I believed she'd sold so the unemployed bottling
plant workers could buy groceries.

Neither Aunt Adeline nor Guthrie were around. Instead, my
niece Sarah Beth, Josie's twelve-year-old daughter, and Darla Bicknell, former line worker, and her four-year old girl, Barrett Leigh,
were in charge.

Sarah Beth held a copy of *Northanger Abbey* and was talking
animatedly to a teenage girl dressed all in black.

"Oh, look at you two all military-like!" Darla exclaimed. In her
late twenties with long strawberry-blonde hair and freckles, she
wasn't in costume but little Barrett Leigh was. She had on a pre-
cious white gown with pink flowers underneath a pink fuzzy coat.
She sat on a folding chair, swinging her legs and drinking lemonade
through a straw.

"Hello, Darla," Flynn said. "Helping Guthrie today?"

"We sure are, Flynn. How are you, Kay? The festival seems to be
off to a great start."

"It does, doesn't it. So exciting," I said. "What have you been up
to?"

"Oh, the usual. Trying to keep Barrett Leigh entertained and working a new job. Miss June at the Golden Age diner is teaching me how to waitress."

"That's great news, Darla," I said. "Are you enjoying it?"

"I am, actually. I like talking to people, and Miss June says that's half the job."

"Were you working when Betsy Bell and Nathaniel came in for lunch last Wednesday?" Flynn asked.

Darla's blue eyes widened. "No, Flynn. I'm part time on the weekends while I learn the ropes. Is-is Betsy Bell, um, is she okay? She made that dress for Barrett Leigh and only charged me the price of the fabric. I know that man was killed with her scissors. Is there anything I can do for her?"

I reached out and touched her arm. "That's so kind of you, Darla. Betsy Bell didn't do anything wrong, so I'm sure she'll be okay."

"It doesn't always work out that way though. Bad things happen to good people," Darla said sadly.

I knew she was thinking of her husband, Foster, who'd broken his back in a car accident.

"But I hope you're right," she said and smiled.

A gentleman was holding a copy of *Emma*. Flynn and I moved away so Darla could help him. As Sarah Beth's customer walked away, I greeted her.

"Aunt Kay, Mr. Holden," Sarah Beth said, dropping a curtsy. She had on a blue print Regency gown and wore a huge paisley shawl over it. "I'm okay. It's just that some of these people aren't true Janeites, and it's exasperating!"

"What do you mean?" I asked.

She let out a dramatic sigh. "That goth girl that was here. She'd seen the *Northanger Abbey* movie—the one with JJ Feild in it—and loved it. She wanted to know which of the other Austen movies were good." Sarah Beth rolled her eyes. "Of course, I told her the 1995 adaptation of *Pride and Prejudice*."

"Of course," I echoed.

"I actually wrote her a list. Then, finally, I convinced her to read one of the books. To be a good Janeite, you must have read the books *and* seen the adaptations," she pronounced.

Flynn chuckled and tossed his empty cup in the trash.

Suddenly, a group of five giggling girls around eighteen years old came rushing up to Flynn. They were each dressed in the latest modern fashions, carrying designer bags, and clearly from out of town.

One of them, a blonde wearing a Tiffany heart necklace, gave Flynn a flirtatious look and breathed, "Maybe you could help me, Captain..."

"Holden."

No problem taking on a fictitious army rank then...

"My friends and I saw *Persuasion* on Netflix. The one with Dakota Johnson. That's how we know about Jane Austen. Then we saw the 2005 movie of *Pride and Prejudice*. We came down on the bus from Philly for this festival and want to be in costume, maybe like Anne Elliott only, you know, prettier. Could you help us?" she said, sidling closer to Flynn.

"Maybe I can *persuade* you to buy the book," Sarah Beth said in a sassy tone Josie would not be happy to hear.

The girls looked at her blankly, then, as one, turned back to Flynn.

He said, "I'm afraid I can't be of assistance, but my friend—"

Another girl interrupted him by squealing. "You have an English accent!"

Darla had finished with her customer and was listening to the girls with a half-smile on her face.

It was time to take charge. "Ladies, you'll find the best Regency gowns at Happy Fabrics. The owner, Miss Ward will be happy to help you. Her sales tent—"

"Oh look! Look!" the blonde shouted. "It's Mr. Darcy!"

Sure enough, a handsome man dressed in Regency clothing and carrying a large sign that read "Mr. Fitzwilliam Darcy" was setting up a Proposal Booth. For five dollars, festival goers could have Mr. Darcy propose marriage to them and then have their picture taken with him.

Without another word, the girls ran over to him, wallets in hand.

"Mr. Darcy is one of the performers from Colonial Williamsburg," Flynn explained.

Sarah Beth snorted and rolled her eyes. "What a bunch of Lydia Bennets."

"Kay, the diner?" Flynn said.

"Yes. Let's go. We'll see you later, Sarah Beth, Karla. Bye-bye, Barrett Leigh."

The little girl waved.

We began walking to the diner but hadn't gotten far when I heard Aunt Adeline's voice call me. She was at Serenity's Art tent.

We stopped and greeted Aunt Adeline and Hayley's mother, an African-American woman in yet another striking caftan, this one in shades of red and orange. Serenity wasn't her real name. Under the Secrets Tree one day, Hayley had confided how her mother had taken on the name after her father, an alcoholic, had finally landed in jail after a vehicular manslaughter conviction. Although Hayley never said so, I had the awful feeling there had been violence in their home when Mr. Conner, who was white, had been drinking. Serenity had wanted to give herself a new name now that she had a fresh start, and found the name Serenity soothing. Serenity preferred to be called just that and never, ever Mrs. Conner.

"Serenity, I'm so pleased that you're doing silhouettes for the festival," I said, looking around the tent. She had four samples of her silhouette work on display as well as animal portraits. She did beautiful portraits of pets; I knew as Aunt Adeline had one of Rama in her bedroom.

"I've had right many commissions already. I guess people find them an unusual way to have a portrait of themselves hanging on the wall. They like the pet portraits too."

A stack of coloring books with men and women in Regency clothing caught my eye. "Where did those come from?

Serenity smiled and passed me one. "You like it?"

I flipped through the pages. "It's great! Did you do this?"

She nodded. "I designed them and had them made up. Thought we needed something extra for the children who are coming to the festival. They come with a sixteen pack of crayons."

"What a lovely idea. I bet they'll be popular with adults too."

"You're right. Coloring helps with stress."

"May I buy one? I know a little girl who'd love this."

"Barrett Leigh?" Flynn asked.

"Yes," I said, digging in my reticule for some money. I paid Serenity and told Flynn I'd be right back. I hurried back to Guthrie's tent and handed Darla the coloring book and crayons.

"This is adorable!" Darla exclaimed. "What do I owe you?"

"Serenity made them up. Isn't it great? And you don't owe me a thing. I've got to run!"

"Thank you, Kay!" Darla called after me.

Aunt Adeline was engaged in speaking with Flynn while Serenity talked to a woman about a possible pet portrait of her poodle, Napoleon.

"Kay," Aunt Adeline said, "Be at the house at two-thirty for the meeting with the attorney. And bring Betsy Bell no matter what."

"Yes ma'am."

"You and Flynn go on to the diner. A few minutes ago, I saw Detective Gordon and Officer Fowler headed in that direction."

Chapter Nine

F lynn opened the door to the Golden Age Diner for me, and I heard Johnny Mercer and The Pied Pipers singing "Accentuate the Positive." Stepping inside, I breathed in the smell of fried chicken and hot biscuits. My gaze took in the Hollywood film posters that covered every inch of the walls. *Casablanca*, *The Maltese Falcon*, *The Adventures of Robin Hood*, *Rear Window*, *Double Indemnity*, *All About Eve*, *Citizen Kane*, *King Kong*, and many more along with the stars themselves in studio portraits.

The poster for the 1940 movie version of *Pride and Prejudice* with Greer Garson as Elizabeth and Laurence Olivier as Mr. Darcy had been decorated with a mini version of the festival banner and a Jane Austen flag underneath. Waitresses dressed in black skirts and gold lamé tops hurried from table to table.

"Look who is having a chat with Francie and Miss June," Flynn said.

Past the gold-colored vinyl booths and round tables with gold Formica tops was a horseshoe shaped booth in the very back next to the kitchen door where Miss June usually held court. In it sat Francie, Miss June, Detective Gordon, and Officer Fowler.

"Detective Gordon and Officer Fowler are getting up to leave," I observed.

At that moment, Chuck Jones from the defunct bottling plant came up to the hostess station where I stood with Flynn. My mouth dropped open to see the former night shift forklift operator. Dressed in black pants and a gold lamé shirt stretched over a hefty middle-aged spread, he gave me a big grin. "Miss Starling, bet you're surprised to see me here. Table for two?"

"Um, no Chuck. We're here to see Francie. But you're right, I am surprised to see you working here. This is Flynn Holden, by the way."

The two men shook hands.

"Good to meet you, Flynn." He gave a hearty laugh that threatened the buttons of his shirt. "I was desperate for a job that wouldn't take me out of Boring, er, I mean Jane Austen Town, and Miss June took me on. I'm happy! No more nights! Peggy Jean doesn't have to tiptoe around the house during the day while I sleep, and I get to hear all the gossip first." He beamed at me.

I smiled. "That's wonderful, Chuck. I saw Darla and she said she's doing weekend shifts."

He nodded. "She's a smart girl and working here will be a good thing for her too what with Foster being out of commission with his back right now."

"You're right about that. Listen, Chuck, we're going back to talk to Francie." I kept an eye on Detective Gordon who was getting ready to walk past us, Officer Fowler behind him.

"See you later, Kay. Nice to meet you, Flynn." Chuck went to wait on a party of four.

"Miss Starling, Mr. Holden," Detective Gordon said.

I missed that he no longer called me Kay. Flynn and I said hello and went to move past him, but he stopped us with his next words.

"I spoke to Mimi Monday, Miss Starling. She told me she couldn't remember what time you left Monday's Country Store the day of the murder."

Officer Fowler, wearing that bright pink lipstick again, said, "That means we only have your word for how long you were gone from the Assembly Rooms and what time you returned. Theoretically, you had plenty of time to kill Nathaniel Playford like you said you wanted to in that text."

My heartbeat sped up. "Except that I didn't kill him," I managed. "What about the women who were at the dancing lesson Nathaniel gave just before he was murdered. Have you checked on them?"

Detective Gordon had a sucked-on-a-lemon expression. "What are you trying to do? Play Miss Marple? Or trying to deflect from your own guilt or that of Mr. Holden's here."

"I'm trying to be of help, that's all. It's the neighborly thing to do," I said, fear and annoyance warring in my head.

"Neither one of us killed Nathaniel, Detective Gordon," Flynn said coldly. "You'll have to look elsewhere."

He gave a slight nod in Officer Fowler's direction. She flipped through her notebook, then said, "Five of the six females were from out of town, the sixth being Miss Scales, the teacher. Five of them had met Nathaniel Playford for the first time that morning. Only Alexandra Bartholomew knew the victim. She claims he gave dancing lessons during her Jane Austen weekend at her B&B in Massachusetts. She considered him part of the help and had very little interaction with him." She shut the notebook.

I didn't believe that statement of Alexandra's for one minute after seeing firsthand her angry exchange with him, but I didn't tell Officer Fowler that.

Flynn took my elbow. "If you'll excuse us, Detective Gordon, Officer Fowler, we wish to speak with friends rather than deny baseless accusations."

Flynn guided me in the direction of where Francie and Miss June sat. I kept thinking that any minute Detective Gordon would call me back, but when I risked a glance back, it was to see the door to the diner closing behind him.

Flynn smiled at Francie. He gave a slight bow to Miss June who sat at the edge of the booth, facing outward, both hands folded at the top of her cane. She had white hair with some gray mixed in, a gentle smile that fooled no one who knew her, and large, brown, owl-like eyes that surveyed her queendom and never missed a trick.

"Miss June," I said as Flynn and I sat in the seat opposite them, "How are you today?"

"Alive!" she said in a strong voice.

"Yes ma'am," I said.

Francie looked amused. She wore her dyed black hair in a short, Louise Brooks bob. Louise was a favorite of Francie. She copied not only the iconic actress's hairstyle, but also her makeup looks of long, thin eyebrows, dark silver-grey eyeshadow, and lipstick in a noir red. "Can I get you anything, Flynn, Kay? Some iced tea?"

I definitely heard Flynn wince.

"No, thank you," he maddeningly spoke for both of us. "We were hoping that you would assist us by answering some questions about Nathaniel Playford."

Miss June banged her cane on the floor and snorted. "The man was smoother than gravy sliding down mashed potatoes. A scoundrel."

Peggy Lee started singing "Why Don't You Do Right" with the Benny Goodman Orchestra.

"Are y'all trying to find out who killed him?" Francie asked, keeping her voice down.

"Why would they? I can't imagine anyone is sorry he's dead," Miss June said in a withering tone.

"We want to help Betsy Bell," I said. "Detective Gordon considers her his prime suspect."

"As if that child could hurt a fly," Miss June scoffed. "And that's what I told Derek Gordon when he asked."

"Betsy Bell and Nathaniel came here for lunch on Wednesday. Did either of you notice anything unusual about their time here?" Flynn asked.

"The fact that they were here together was unusual," Miss June proclaimed staunchly. "But, that's our Betsy Bell all over. Naïve as a baby. I heard Nathaniel ask her if she would come back to his room at the Farmhouse Inn and sew a button on his breeches.

Innocent as she is, I think Betsy Bell went back there with him. I didn't tell Derek that though."

"I'm glad you didn't tell him, Miss June." Although I had a feeling he'd find out.

"How the creature ever came to our town is beyond me," Miss June said. "He came in here for lunch more than once and never left a tip. The type of man that squeezes a quarter so hard the eagle screams."

Flynn held out his hands in an apologetic gesture. "I'm to blame, I'm afraid. I knew him slightly from working with him in Colonial Williamsburg. I had no idea he was such a miscreant or I never would have recommended him to be our dancing master. I apologize."

Miss June gave a sharp nod of acceptance.

I looked at Francie, noticing her charm bracelet that had little picture frames filled with photos of male Golden Age movie stars. "Francie, I'm sorry to pry, but you had dinner with Nathaniel that night, didn't you?"

"Don't worry, Kay, I understand." She moved the little picture frames on the bracelet around for a minute, then said, "I met Nathaniel at Starling's Grocery store. He asked me my advice on the freshness of an avocado. We got to talking about food and he asked me to have dinner with him."

"Had you seen him here at the diner with Betsy Bell?" Flynn asked.

"No. I'd left after the breakfast rush. Anyway, I only agreed to go to dinner with him because he seemed like just a friendly guy at the grocery store. New to town, trying to meet people." She gave me a pleading look.

"I'm certain he could be charming when he wanted to be," I assured her.

"Men who secretly hate women always are," Miss June stated.

Francie continued. "He took me to the Farmhouse Inn restaurant. Within ten minutes I could tell he was a creep. The kind of guy Robert Mitchum would have taken out with one punch in one of his movies. When we got our menus, see, Nathaniel told me he was sure I'd be willing to pay for dinner. Like I'd be so grateful for the honor of his company." Francie rolled her eyes. "I got up and left."

"I'm glad you did," I said, my face hot with anger at Francie being treated that way.

"Who do you think killed him?" Miss June asked.

"We don't know, but are doing everything we can to find out," Flynn said grimly.

Miss June's eyes narrowed. "Have you talked with that snob, Alexandra Bartholomew? My money's on her. I saw them in Dogwood Park on Tuesday morning when I went for my walk. They were stuck together like lettuce covered in salad dressing. Had Francie told me she planned to go to dinner with him, I would have forbidden it," Miss June said.

Francie picked at the polish on her blood red fingernails.

"That's a good lead," Flynn said. "Thank you, Miss June."

We slid out of the booth.

Miss June rose. "I've got to make my rounds. My customers expect me to talk with them." She ambled away.

She meant gossip with them.

"Francie, thank you too," I said.

Francie stood, looked around, then spoke in a low voice. "Look, Betsy Bell is honey-sweet and we all know she's on the naïve side like Grandmother said."

"Right," Flynn said.

"I'm not one to gossip and you didn't hear this from me, but let me tell you," Francie let out a heavy sigh. "Betsy Bell has never had a boyfriend that I know of. I think that if she did go back to the Farmhouse Inn with Nathaniel and...well, something happened between them that Betsy Bell wasn't bargaining for, that maybe she freaked out and killed him the next day. It was her scissors he was stabbed with. I heard you two were the only other people there and neither of you did it, so it had to be Betsy Bell. It's the only thing that makes sense." Francie said with finality.

"Oh, I don't think so," I said, appalled at the theory.

"That's what happened in a film noir I saw once," Francie said. "You can't rule her out."

Chuck walked over with his order pad in hand and a questioning look directed at Francie.

Flynn and I said goodbye to them.

Outside, I turned my face to the afternoon sun. Despite the warmth, I'd had a chill at Francie's words.

"Francie has a point," Flynn said as if reading my mind.

"There's no way that Betsy Bell killed Nathaniel. I won't believe it."

"Then who did? You and Betsy Bell were the only two there."

My temper went from zero to sixty. "So, if it wasn't Betsy Bell, it was me that killed him, is that what you're saying?"

He looked into my eyes and neither of us said anything for a moment.

Flynn broke the silence. "Kay, if you had anything to do with it, perhaps helped her in the heat of the moment over his threat to the festival, I will get you the best criminal defense attorney in Virginia."

"How kind! That's what you think of me? Maybe *you* should get an attorney. You're the one who knew him in Colonial Williamsburg. You have a history with him. You're the one who brought him here. You're the one who materialized from the kitchen minutes after he was killed. Who knows how long you'd been in there!"

Flynn glanced at people who were looking our way. "Keep your voice down. "I had no reason to wish Nathaniel harm. None."

"We don't really that though, do we?" I said, seething. "You're an outsider for all that you own the community center and Pete Holden's historic estate."

"I see you've taken offense at my offer."

Master of the understatement!

My phone chimed. I took it out of my reticule with shaking hands. It was a reminder from Aunt Adeline to get Betsy Bell to the house to meet with Brock Winthrop in thirty minutes. I tucked my phone away.

"As it happens, Aunt Adeline has set up a meeting with an attorney to speak to Betsy Bell at Starling Farm. Betsy Bell's selling Regency dresses at her tent. I need to find someone to relieve her for an hour or so. If you'll excuse me."

No sooner had I turned away then his hand came to rest on my back.

"May I come with you to the meeting?" he asked.

I started walking faster towards Betsy Bell's tent so his hand dropped away. "No, I don't think so. Aunt Adeline specified just myself and Betsy Bell."

He let out a low laugh. "Does she suspect me as well?"

I said nothing. I felt ashamed that I'd lost my temper.

"Right. I'll go speak with Mimi Monday and find out exactly what she told Detective Gordon about the timing of your visit before the murder."

"If you wish."

"Or, if you don't already have someone in mind, I could mind Betsy Bell's tent while the two of you are meeting the attorney."

Was he trying to make amends? I'd been so focused on the murder that I'd forgotten to ask anyone for help while Betsy Bell and I were with Brock Winthrop.

"What do you know about women's Regency gowns? Do you know muslin?" I asked.

Before he could answer, our attention was drawn by the sound of raised voices. We'd almost reached Betsy Bell's tent. I saw the tent had been arranged with the colorful, hand-stitched Regency gowns she'd made over the past three months and accessories hanging on a simple display.

Across the way, I saw that Alexandra Bartholomew had a richly appointed tent complete with brocade curtains and an Oriental rug spread across the ground inside. A small area was devoted to information about Jane Austen weekends at her B&B. The majority of space was an exhibition of pastel-colored, plain Regency gowns for sale. They were all the same except for the color.

Betsy Bell, wearing a period-drama ready gold silk Regency gown with copper-colored embroidery and a matching high-crowned silk bonnet, stood in the walkway between the two tents with her arms crossed, glaring at Alexandra. Clad in a tight, hot pink short dress which revealed every curve, Alexandra looked down her nose at Betsy Bell.

"I said, I didn't think it was nice of you to sell those dresses across from my tent," Betsy Bell declared.

"You people in this town are so uneducated. Have you never heard the word capitalism, dear?" Alexandra scoffed.

"Don't you dare insult Jane Austen Town, you...you floozy!" Betsy Bell's normal soft, gentle voice rose. "And I'm not your dear!"

Alexandra stood with her hands on her hips and glared at Betsy Bell. "You're jealous because Nathaniel and I were seeing one another."

"I am not!"

"Kay, you'd better say something to Betsy Bell. People are gawking," Flynn said.

At that moment, Hayley came striding towards us. "What's going on?"

I didn't have time to answer. I made my way to Betsy Bell's side. "Hey, hon, I need you to come with me—"

Betsy Bell ignored me. Her gloved hands balled into fists at her sides, she yelled at Alexandra. "I'm mad because you're selling cheap, polyester dresses *with zippers* that you bought online and brought to our festival to sell for three times the price! You're cheating people!"

Alexandra went red which didn't look great with the hot pink dress. She reached behind her. When she turned back around, I saw she had a half-full bottle of Hurdee Gurdee soda in her hand. She flung the bottle's contents at Betsy Bell. The soda splashed all over Betsy Bell's beautiful dress, staining it.

The small crowd around us gasped.

Betsy Bell had reared back in shock, but now she burst forward with a six-inch floral silk folding fan in her hand. "Oh, my sweet cheese and rice! Look what you've done to my dress!" Faster than thought, she struck Alexandra's arm with the fan, the sticks holding it together promptly breaking into pieces.

Alexandra screamed, then reached out to snatch Betsy Bell's bonnet.

"Oh, no you don't!" Hayley roared. "Not that bonnet. Not today!"

Hayley grasped Alexandra and backed her inside her tent. Alexandra fell onto a chair, rubbing her arm.

"Don't even try to say that little fan hurt you," Hayley warned her.

I put my arm around Betsy Bell who was breathing heavily. "Don't worry about Alexandra. Let's go to my house. We can change your gown and sponge this one with club soda."

"Kay's right, Betsy Bell," Flynn said. "The workmanship of your gowns speaks for itself. You have no competition. I'll mind your tent while you go with Kay."

"Thank you, Flynn. I don't know what came over me. I've just been so on-edge since, well, *you know*." Betsy Bell started to cry.

The crowd was clearly on Betsy Bell's side as several women began examining her gowns for sale. They were more than happy to have the tall, handsome, uniformed Flynn help them.

It was when I went to lead Betsy Bell away that I saw Detective Gordon and Officer Fowler standing to one side, having witnessed the whole altercation.

Chapter Ten

"Well now, Miss Ward, Miss Starling, I think I've got the gist of what happened the day Mr. Playford, or rather, Mr. Grant, was murdered, and Detective Gordon's questioning of you both at the police station," Brock Winthrop said. "And you've told me about Mr. Grant's visit to your store, Miss Ward," he paused and consulted notes he'd written on a yellow legal pad, "Happy Fabrics, to find a button, as well as the lunch you shared the day before at The Golden Age Diner."

Betsy Bell, wearing one of my Regency dresses while Ida Calhoun sponged her gown, had looked downcast, but slowly became more comfortable with the attorney.

We sat around the polished mahogany table in the green formal dining room at Starling Farm. Aunt Adeline had lit the fire in the fireplace, more for a relaxing atmosphere, I think, than for warmth. A teapot, cups, saucers, and dessert plates in the Royal Albert Old Country Roses pattern shone in the sunshine coming in from the tall windows. Aunt Adeline passed around a plate containing slices of banana bread, zucchini bread, and pumpkin bread.

Brock Winthrop was bald and in his fifties, with an air of thoughtful focus and alertness. He wore an expensive gray suit, crisp white Oxford shirt, and a red bow tie.

"What I'd like next, Miss Ward, is for you to tell me what happened after your lunch with Mr. Grant," he said.

Betsy Bell hesitated, then said, "It takes some getting used to hearing him called Mr. Grant. I keep thinking you're talking about someone else."

Mr. Winthrop nodded. "Then let's just call him Nathaniel."

"Okay," Betsy Bell said. "Nathaniel asked me if I would mind sewing the button on his breeches for him back at his room at the Farmhouse Inn. Him being a man and all, he didn't know how to sew, you see."

I saw Aunt Adeline close her eyes and press her fingers to her forehead.

To his credit, Mr. Winthrop kept an expression of professional interest on his face. "And did you agree to go with him?"

"I did. I'd never been inside the Farmhouse Inn, although Kay took me to their restaurant for my birthday last summer. I'd heard the Inn was super nice. It's an expensive place, not somewhere I'd normally go. I was in awe of the antiques they have and the little refrigerator in the room. It was the cutest thing," Betsy Bell said, smiling as she remembered. "I couldn't get over it. It's amazing what they can make nowadays."

"Sure is," Aunt Adeline said. Then a look of alarm came over her face. "Cho! What are you doing down here? Get down! Leave that painting alone."

The cat had jumped up on a chair and reached a paw out to tap a painting of dogs inspecting a rabbit's burrow.

"Is that an Arthur Wardle?" Brock asked, admiration tinting his voice.

"Yes. *Irish and Wire Fox Terriers inspecting a Burrow.*" Aunt Adeline said. "Come on, Cho you can't be seen in public." She picked him up and, ignoring his meows of protest, carried him back upstairs.

"Sorry for the interruption," I said. "Cho is new to our family. Aunt Adeline wants to keep him upstairs until he adjusts."

But why did Aunt Adeline say Cho couldn't be seen in public? What was it about Cho and his unusual eyes that Aunt Adeline wasn't telling me?

As soon as Aunt Adeline returned, Mr. Winthrop indicated that Betsy Bell should continue.

"After I sewed the button for him, I made Nathaniel show me the inside of the refrigerator. Nathaniel kept calling it a mini-bar, but I think he was wrong about that. I opened it and pulled out every one of the cans inside as well as some candy bars and there wasn't any alcohol." Betsy Bell searched our faces as if seeking affirmation that the dancing master had been wrong.

I was thinking of the mini-bar charge Nathaniel would have faced and held back a snort. Of course, being dead, he didn't have to worry about it.

"Go on," Mr. Winthrop said.

"That's it, really," Betsy Bell said with a shrug. "I had just seen a television set on the bathroom wall, if you can believe that, when Nathaniel said he remembered he had an appointment. He showed me to the door and opened it with one of those bows he does—did—and said, 'Good day to you,' and I left and walked back to my store."

"Now, I'd like to hear about the spat you had with Alexandra Bartholomew," Mr. Winthrop said to Betsy Bell.

With my help, Betsy Bell told him what happened ending with, "I shouldn't have lost my temper, but Alexandra's dishonest. It's not right."

"Not to mention that there were no zippers in the Regency period. They hadn't been invented yet," I said.

Aunt Adeline gave me a look that plainly said, "Now is not the time for lessons in historical accuracy."

Mr. Winthrop studied Betsy Bell. "Do you often struggle with holding your temper?"

"Not at all," Betsy Bell said. "Mama always taught me that a lady should be quiet and not cause a fuss. Daddy wouldn't stand for raised voices in the house."

"Mr. and Mrs. Ward were older when Betsy Bell was born," Aunt Adeline said. "They live in a retirement community in Florida now."

"I see," Mr. Winthrop said, making notes. Then he put his pen down. "Miss Ward, I think I have all the information I need for now. I'll stop by the police station and let them know I'm representing you. In the meantime, I must stress that you're not to talk to Detective Gordon, Officer Fowler, or any other law enforcement personnel without my presence. If they want to interview you again, they should call me. If they approach you, or if you have any questions, call me," he said, passing her his business card.

"Thank you, Mr. Winthrop," Betsy Bell said. "Do you need my address to send me a bill?"

Aunt Adeline said, "Don't worry about that, Betsy Bell. You'd best go back to your sales tent and relieve Flynn. Let's go out the back door so we can pick up your Regency gown. Hopefully, Ida got the stain out."

As Aunt Adeline led Betsy Bell away, I checked my phone. There was a text from Hayley.

"Flynn convinced Alexandra not to press charges against Betsy Bell for hitting her with that little fan."

I waited for Aunt Adeline to return then said, "I have to tell you both that Detective Gordon and Officer Fowler witnessed the altercation between Betsy Bell and Alexandra. When Betsy Bell and I left the area, the detective was on his phone and Officer Fowler had her notebook out. One piece of good news; I've been informed that Alexandra will not be pressing charges against Betsy Bell."

"Over something so small, she'd be laughed out of court, but it's unfortunate that law enforcement witnessed the event," Mr. Winthrop said. "Miss Ward is not in a good position, and displaying her temper like that makes it worse. Mind you, I don't think she killed this man. I'm prepared to defend her, if need be."

"It would be nice if someone else is arrested for the murder," Aunt Adeline said. "An outsider."

"I have the notes you gave me about possible suspects. I'd like to know more about Alexandra since she too showed that she had a temper in the altercation with Miss Ward. There's also the scent of her perfume at the murder scene and her alleged angry words with the victim. Clearly, they had been romantically involved as Alexandra admitted as much during the argument with Miss Ward," he said.

"I'm going to track her down in the morning and see what I can find out," I said.

"I can't approve of your sleuthing, but do let me know what you find out," he said with a smile. Then he fixed me with a stern look. "I would give you the same advice that I gave Miss Ward. Do not speak to law enforcement without me. I'm representing you as well, Miss Starling, if that's agreeable, of course."

"Yes, I appreciate it. Thank you," I said. "Hopefully it won't be necessary."

The attorney packed his legal pad in his laptop backpack. "Don't discount anything," he warned. The murder is all over the Charlottesville news websites. National news sites will pick it up soon enough, if they haven't already. Detective Gordon will be under pressure to make an arrest. Keep your guard up."

Aunt Adeline showed him to the door.

I Googled the Charlottesville newspaper and sure enough the top story screamed, "Murder at the Jane Austen Festival!" They knew Nathaniel Playford was actually Nathaniel Grant, too.

I reached for a piece of pumpkin bread and stress-ate it. Then I picked up a piece of banana bread.

"Kay," Aunt Adeline said. "I see by the way you're devouring that bread that the news of the murder is on the net."

I groaned. "I don't know what I thought would happen. The news was bound to get out."

"There's nothing we can do about it. It's almost four o'clock. We need to get down to the Promenade. Are you coming to the talk on Jane's life tonight or going to the *Sense & Sensibility* screening at the theater?"

"I'm not sure," I said as we walked out the front door and down the driveway. "I may stay home and come up with a plan of action for tomorrow."

"All right. Keep your wits about you if you're out after dark. A murderer could be among our midst."

"Yes, ma'am."

We reached the end of the driveway. Aunt Adeline glanced around with approval. "Oh my, look. Everyone is gathering. They'll walk from the Village Green all down Main Street and then back. Here, I'll let you go on. I want to see if Guthrie is at his shop. Text me later and let me know your plans."

She hurried away.

I walked closer to the Village Green and took in the scene, my heart lifting at the spectacular sight before me.

Miss Austen's Militia began the Promenade along with musicians including a drummer. A piper began playing as I looked for Flynn. When I spotted him among a sea of redcoats, I saw that his eyes were on me. He tipped his cocked hat and smiled at me, his gaze lingering before he marched with the other men and the militia ladies.

He looked uber-hot in his uniform. Okay, he was handsome in anything he wore. But I wasn't attracted to him. Absolutely not. Hadn't he suggested that I might have had a hand in Nathaniel's death only hours before? Get ahold of yourself, Kay.

Next came Mayor Buckalew, in costume, with Coralie Buchard in a coral-colored Regency dress. They grinned and waved. Actually, the mayor grinned, but Coralie had an impatient look on her face.

Neil walked beside the crowd, taking photographs for the *Jane Austen Town Gazette*.

The participants swept up Main Street, more than half of them in costume. Ladies dressed in colorful Regency gowns, carrying basket purses or reticules, wearing bonnets, or modern headbands, their necks encircled with pearls or beads of coral or turquoise. As the day had grown chilly, many ladies wore shawls. Gentlemen dressed in a variety of historical coats and breeches or regular slacks. One man dressed in a Pomona-green coat and tan breeches pushed a stroller. Another wore jeans and a flannel shirt. Children wove through the crowd waving miniature Union Jack flags.

I felt tears threaten, but they were tears of joy. There must have been three hundred people.

Then I laughed out loud as Hugo came into view driving a carriage. He wore his Regency costume with top hat. Next to him, sitting tall, was Bowie wearing his matching top hat, his pink tongue hanging out in between excited woofs. Hugo drove an open carriage, a landau, with the Philly girls I'd met earlier giggling and waving handkerchiefs. I noted they wore the ice cream color gowns sold by Alexandra. There was a sign on the side of the carriage which read: Carriage Rides in Dogwood Park.

As the carriage passed and a few people dawdled, my heart almost stopped in my chest. A man stood on the sidewalk, his hand shading his eyes from the setting sun, looking around for someone. When he saw me, he started in my direction.

It was Jonathan Warren from Dale Casino Resorts.

Chapter Eleven

"Miz Starling, the look on your face says that if you were a snake you'd have bit me before I crossed the street," Jonathan said, the boyish smile once again on his face and his dimples creased his cheeks.

He wore cowboy boots with dark jeans and a white shirt with pearl snaps. His thick, ash-blond hair was combed back, and his chocolate brown eyes had the audacity to twinkle.

"Mr. Warren," I said, my tone dripping ice. "What brings you to Jane Austen Town?"

"Silas Dale, my boss, instructed me to come down and see what was going on with the town after he learned of the murder," Jonathan said frankly.

"He thinks he can swoop down here now and get his way with the casino."

"Yes, I believe that's his thinking. He wants me to assess the situation. I drove down from New Jersey this morning and am staying in Charlottesville. There wasn't anywhere closer that had a vacancy."

"I suppose you and your boss are happy at the turn of events, but as you can see from the Promenade, Jane Austen Town is doing fine."

He shook his head slowly. "You're wrong about me. Okay, Silas is rubbing his hands with glee, but I'm not. A man lost his life. That's not a business opportunity. Besides, I believe the people of this town have spoken. That should be respected." He looked toward the Promenade which was working its way back up Main Street to us. "The casino resort wouldn't work unless the people here *wanted* it to."

Lorraine Longo appeared at my side. She took a step back when she realized who I was talking to. "Um, Kay, can I speak with you for a minute?"

Jonathan said hello to her and politely walked a few paces away to give us privacy.

"Isn't he one of the casino people?" Lorraine whispered.

"Yes, his boss sent him to see what was going on."

She stole a quick glance at Jonathan. "He looks harmless enough. Cute too."

"I don't know if he's harmless yet. What's up, Lorraine?"

"I heard about the fight between Betsy and Alexandra. I want you to know that I never would have assigned Alexandra her tent across from Betsy Bell's if I'd known she was selling dresses. Alexandra told me her tent would be about her B & B in Massachusetts. She'd be there to hand out pamphlets and answer questions. She never mentioned any dresses for sale, Kay."

"So, she lied."

"It would seem she did."

"Don't worry, Lorraine. You didn't do anything wrong. Where's Eric?"

"He's home with the kids." She brushed a stray hair from her face. "I should go. Eric's promised to fix dinner, but I'd better be there to supervise. Last time, Eric gave the kids pop tarts with their chicken and broccoli. Guess which one they ended up eating," she said with a smile. Then, "You watch yourself with that one." She tilted her head toward Jonathan and then walked away.

In the fading light, I saw Miss Austen's Militia winding toward where I stood on the Village Green. As they grew closer, Flynn shot me a look that went from surprise to suspicion, so unlike the expression of happiness he'd given me when the Promenade started. He turned his face away sharply.

What now? Did he think I was in cahoots with the casino people since the festival had been tainted by a murder?

"Miz Starling, you look real pale," Jonathan said, back at my side. "Have you eaten lately? I'm so hungry my stomach feels like my throat's been cut. Will you go with me for a bite to eat?"

Coralie Bouchard, walking with the mayor, dashed over to us. "Why Jonathan Warren, it's nice to see you back in Boring," she gushed grasping Jonathan's hand.

I guess she'd forgotten the town had been renamed.

"Nice to see you again, ma'am," he replied.

I could tell he couldn't remember her name.

The mayor loudly cleared his throat.

"I have to run but don't be a stranger," she said to Jonathan. "Come see me while you're here."

She totally ignored me.

"Word's going to be all around town within the hour that you've been seen consorting with the enemy," Jonathan teased. "You might as well keep me company over a meal, don't you think?"

Why not? I could find out more about him and more about Silas Dale's plans. "All right. Where would you like to go?"

"Since Main Street is closed to vehicles, my car's parked at a big grass parking lot in front of a place called Gator's. Do you know it? I've not eaten there myself."

"Oh, yes, it's quite the gourmet experience."

He narrowed his eyes at me. "Why Miz Starling, I believe you're joshing me."

I chuckled. "Call me Kay."

The town had gone blue with twilight. The white lights in the greenery decorating houses and businesses, along with the people in costume, gave a magical air to Jane Austen Town. We walked west of Main Street all the way down Elm Street. We passed clapboard, two story houses with lights burning inside and people watching TV or enjoying their evening meal. We turned at the corner of Possum Trot Road.

Built in the 1930s, Gator's was a small, dark brown, clapboard building with an A-frame front porch on a brick foundation. Four tables and chairs were set outside, but none were occupied as the temperature had dropped. Across the width of the A-frame roof, the word Gator's was spelled out in neon red. Cars were parked in the grassy area with a few parked on the side of the building, including Gator's 1968 Pontiac Bonneville. A sign in the window and another on the front door read, "CASH ONLY."

A big, light brown dog of uncertain parentage bounded off the porch to greet us.

"Hey there, Tater," I said, bending to stroke his chest and shoulders. He wagged his tail with pleasure.

"Tater?" Jonathan said. Then to the dog, "Who's a good boy?"

Tater snuffled and gave a short, high-pitched bark, then ran back to the porch where he had a big dog bed waiting for him. He had another inside for when he got cold.

"Yes, his name is Tater, and he's a sweet dog," I said as Jonathan opened the door to the bar for me. I noticed that he was wearing one of the white wristbands that confirmed he'd bought a ticket to the festival. "You'll see why Gator calls him that."

Inside, the lighting was dim with multicolored Christmas lights strung across the bar and where the walls met the ceiling. They were there year-round.

A jukebox playing Greg Allman's "Midnight Rider" stood in a corner. Groups of small tables with laminated brown tops marched on either side of an aisle that led to the bar. A TV screen showing a football game hung from the right side of the bar. The power strip was loose and dangling down. The walls were mostly covered with signs for various brands of beer, but the main decoration was plastic alligators. Some life size, some smaller, they hung in fishing nets.

"We can sit anywhere," I told Jonathan. "Gator will know we're here."

Heads turned as we walked through the bar. I knew word of our appearance together would be around town in minutes.

Jonathan seemed unconcerned as he looked around. "This place reminds me of dive bars in my home state of Texas. Wait, is that the menu?"

"I was wondering when you'd catch on," I said as we sat underneath a sign that read, "Today's Special: Buy Two Drinks and Pay for Them Both."

Up on a blackboard above the bar were the scrawled words, "Tater Tots; Cheesy Tator Tots; Tater Tots Sandwich; Tater Tots Macaroni and Cheese (Regular or XTRA Special)."

"That's why the dog is named Tater," Jonathan said leaning toward me. "The owner loves tater tots."

"Exactly. And here comes Gator. Hope you know what you want to eat. Oh, and he only serves beer and water to drink."

Gator strolled lazily up to the table. He was of average height but thin and bony. His long, thick blond hair was held in a ponytail by a rubber band. He wore flip-flops, faded jeans, and a T-shirt that pictured an alligator and the word "Later." A beaded necklace of white howlite and green malachite was his only adornment.

He greeted me by lifting his chin in my direction. His gaze went to Jonathan for a moment, but returned to me. "Whatcha havin'?"

"Hey, Gator. May I have the regular Tater Tots Macaroni and Cheese and a glass of water, please?"

He gave a slight inclination of his head and looked at Jonathan.

"Um, I'll have the same only have you got a Shiner Bock?"

Gator pointed to the cooler behind the bar.

Jonathan craned his neck to see the bottles of beer and his mouth slanted for a moment. Then, "I'll have a Coors Light."

Without another word, Gator turned and walked back behind the bar into the kitchen.

"Not much of a talker, is he?" Jonathan asked.

"No."

"What's in the back room?"

"A pool table," I answered taking out my cell phone. "I have to send a quick text to my aunt to let her know where I am." I texted Aunt Adeline that I was at Gator's but didn't mention who was with me.

"I see a dart board on that back wall. Can I challenge you to a quick game?"

"Why sure," I said.

He was a good player with great aim, consistently scoring high, but I was better. Ten minutes later we were back at the table where Cherry, Gator's only waitress, placed our food and drinks on the table along with plastic cups. I didn't know if Cherry was her real name or not, but her hair was dyed a cherry-red and she favored a pin-up style of 1950s clothing.

"Hey, Kay, how's everything going with the festival?" she asked me, but her gaze lingered on Jonathan. He smiled at her politely.

"Going great," I said enthusiastically.

"That's nice," she said, flipping her polka-dotted skirt and winking at Jonathan before walking away.

The Doors' "Riders on the Storm" began playing.

We ate in silence for a few minutes, then Jonathan remarked that the food was surprisingly good.

"It's a carb bomb, but sometimes you need that," I said. I tilted my head. "How do I know that you didn't come down here and kill Nathaniel Grant to ruin the festival's business?"

He tensed. "Whoa. Where did that come from?"

"You're not supposed to answer a question with a question."

His face softened. "You care so much, don't you? About Jane Austen Town, that is."

I nodded. "I grew up here. The town's people are my friends, my neighbors."

He pulled out his phone and began tapping. A few minutes went by while I ate and he scrolled. Finally, he turned the screen to me. "This is security footage from Dale Casino Resorts. Here I am walking through the casino *in New Jersey* last night. I'm in the sports betting area. You can tell it was Thursday night because the San Francisco 49ers were playing the Seattle Seahawks."

I looked at the video. Jonathan, dressed in a well-tailored suit, walked behind a line of people seated around a long, curved bar. A row of TV screens, all with the identical view of the game, were mounted above them.

"I don't know much about football," I said.

"But you can see the team names and scores on the scorebug, the graphic, at the bottom of the TV screens," he said.

"Okay, yes, I see it."

He withdrew his phone. "Now Google the game."

I did. He was right. A mixture of embarrassment and relief washed over me. "Could you send me that footage? I'm sorry. Everyone is a suspect until I can identify the killer." I gave him my cell phone number. It only took a few seconds for him to send it.

His eyebrows came together and he looked at me squarely in the eyes. In a low, serious voice he said, "You're going to identify the killer? Kay, why are you doing the job of the police? It's dangerous."

Before I could answer, a movement caught my eye. Detective Gordon walked up to our table. "Good evening, Miss Starling, Mr. Warren."

Jonathan stood and shook his hand.

"What brings you back to town, Mr. Warren?"

"Think of me as a reporter, Detective. My boss wants a report on how the festival is doing since Mr. Grant's death. I was elected to prepare it for him. I can't say I'm mad about it either." He looked at me. "I'm finding the experience charming."

Heat came into my face.

Detective Gordon looked at me. "I hear your friend, Miss Ward, has lawyered up. Can't say that's a bad idea after this afternoon's altercation. In your opinion, were they fighting more over Mr. Grant than the dresses?"

He still thought Betsy Bell was responsible for Nathaniel's death! "I'm afraid that my own attorney has instructed me not to talk about the case to the police without him."

He looked grim at those words. We had all been friends before this happened, or at least I thought we'd been friends. Maybe he was regretting the turn of events. Or maybe now that he knew he didn't have a chance with Hayley, he'd become more ambitious in his career.

"Fine," he said tightly. "I'll speak to Mr. Holden, since he was there, and take a statement. Although, I don't know how impartial he will be since Mr. Grant stole Mr. Holden's girlfriend from him back in Williamsburg."

What? He did what?

"Have a good evening," Detective Gordon said and walked away, nodding and speaking to people on his way out.

I sat stunned. Why hadn't Flynn told me about this woman? Had it been serious? Was he hurt? My heart beat faster. Hurt enough to kill Nathaniel?

"Kay," Jonathan said, sitting opposite me once more. "Are you all right? I realize we don't know each other hardly at all, but I'm concerned. What just happened confirms my belief that you should leave the murder investigation to the police."

I barely heard him. "It seems Nathaniel Grant was not only quite the playboy, but also the sort of man who relished riling people, dividing them. Probably gave him a sense of power."

Jonathan sighed and put his napkin down. "Okay, I give in. Tell me about this altercation the detective was asking about."

While he ate his cooling food, I filled him in on what happened between Betsy Bell and Alexandra. He was a good listener and asked questions.

"You say it was a dainty, little hand fan and no one is pressing charges?"

"That's right."

"Betsy Bell can be ruled out as a suspect, but I'm not sure about this Alexandra woman. Sounds like she was fixin' to escalate the physical side of the argument. Is there anyone else you suspect?"

"Maybe. I have reason to believe Nathaniel had been married at some point. He didn't wear a wedding ring. No one seems to know about his wife or ex-wife if they're divorced. Detective Gordon probably knows who she is but I don't. I wish I did, and I wish I knew where she was now."

"I can help with that, but honestly, I don't want to encourage your sleuthing. I mean it, Kay. Whoever it is, the killer was bold enough to act in broad daylight, in a place where anyone could have walked in on him or her."

I disregarded his warning. "How could you find out who Nathaniel's wife was?"

"I can't talk you out of this?"

I shook my head no.

He let out a breath. "I could run a background check on him via the casino. Their checks are very thorough, trust me."

"Would you? Would you help us?" I ask excitedly.

"I shouldn't consider it, but I'll do it for you. Don't ever tell Silas Dale, though, as I'll lose my job, okay?"

"Deal."

He tapped on his phone, then set it on the table. "It'll take a few minutes."

"Thank you, Jonathan."

He shrugged. "What can I say? It's the Texan in me. I don't like to see a pretty lady in distress."

I realized our whole conversation had been focused on my concerns. "I haven't asked about you. Do you like working for Silas Dale? He doesn't seem to be a very nice person if you don't mind me saying so."

He laughed. "No, he's not. But he's a successful businessman, and I've learned a lot from him. Not that casino work was what I saw myself doing when I was growing up."

"What did you want to do?"

"Oh, I had some crazy ideas. When you grow up in Houston, you're aware of the Johnson Space Center. When I was a little boy, I always watched launches on TV. My daddy took me on the Mission Control Tour." He chuckled. "I wanted to build space shuttles to Mars."

I smiled. "What happened?"

"I thought I could get into aerospace engineering, but then life happened as it so often does. My parents were killed in a small plane crash. I had to take care of my little sister. A buddy of mine was moving to Las Vegas to work at a casino. He got me a job, so I took Jessica and moved. I did well, moved up to management, and met Silas Dale at an industry convention."

I studied him. "Something tells me you'd still like to build that space shuttle."

He gave me a sheepish smile. "I'll tell you a secret. I work with a charity that helps underprivileged kids go to the Breakfast with an

Astronaut program at the Johnson Space Center. Kids should be able to dream."

"And Jessica? Is she doing okay?"

"She's at Vassar on a scholarship, majoring in economics. We meet in the City, and I take her shopping. I'd like to move back South at some point, but not while she's in New York."

Cherry came and cleared our plates. "Everything all right?"

Jonathan's phone dinged.

I smiled at Cherry. "Fine, thank you."

Unable to get Jonathan's attention, she headed back to the kitchen.

He looked up at me. "Nathaniel's ex-wife. She's local. Sharon Calhoun Grant. Do you know her?"

Chapter Twelve

"Kay Starling! I am most seriously displeased!"

I shot up to a sitting position in bed with the same speed as if I'd found Mr. Collins next to me spouting one of his little delicate compliments with an unstudied air. "Hayley! I thought you were Lady Catherine speaking, and that led me to think of Mr. Collins."

"Most unfortunate, but we are not role-playing *Pride and Prejudice*," she said, sitting on the bed next to me. She had on a marigold yellow, muslin Regency gown with a matching headdress and a determined look on her face. "Don't try to distract me from the fact that you were out partying with Jonathan Warren last night."

I rubbed the sleep from my eyes and laid back down, trying to pull my Jane Austen quilt over me but Hayley was sitting on it. "If you call stuffing my face with tater tots at Gator's with Jonathan 'partying,' then I plead guilty. What time is it?" I asked with a yawn.

"Quarter to eight. How could you spend time with a man who works with Silas Dale? Remember him? The guy who wants to destroy our town? How do you know his minion didn't kill Nathaniel in hopes of destroying our festival?"

"I had the same thought, but it isn't true. Hand me my phone, please."

Hayley reached over to my night table, picked up my phone, and passed it to me. I took the opportunity to draw the quilt around me. My long, white Regency nightgown wasn't enough to battle my bedroom's morning's chill.

At that moment, Cho sauntered into the room, studied us for a moment, then jumped on the bed, inspecting Hayley thoroughly.

Hayley gasped. "Look at hiiiiiiimm," she cried, reaching out and gently running her hand from his ears down his back. "Jane Pawsten would be whiskers over tail in love if she saw this handsome fella."

Cho seemed to appreciate her compliments as he nudged her hand with his head and purred.

"All right, Hayley. Look at this," I said extending the phone to her. "Press play. It's Jonathan at the New Jersey casino. You can tell it was Thursday night because the, um, San Francisco 49ers were playing the Seattle Seagulls. Um no, Seahawks, that's it."

Hayley watched the security footage. "Since when do you know anything about football?"

"I googled it."

Cho moved away from Hayley, positioned himself at the end of my Jane Austen quilt, then tunneled underneath it.

"Hmm, it does seem unlikely that Jonathan would drive through the night to come down here, then hang around looking for Nathaniel, then kill him. But what's he doing here in Jane Austen Town?"

I sat forward and hugged my knees. "He was upfront about it. He told me that Silas Dale assigned him the task of keeping an eye on the festival now that there's been a murder and report back to him."

"Because Silas Dale thinks the festival will fail, and he can swoop in and get his way about the casino."

"Exactly."

"Ugh. Silas Dale is messier than a jelly donut put in the microwave too long," Hayley said.

"Jonathan doesn't seem to like him much. Plus, Jonathan's really nice, Hayley. He's taken care of his younger sister since their parents died. And he's involved with a charity in Texas for underprivileged kids. He said he wants to move back to the South at some point."

Hayley's eyebrows rose. "I believe you like Mr. Warren, Kay. Sounds like you had a big time with him at Gator's. You're not falling for his dimples, are you? What would Flynn say?"

"Oh, my stars in heaven, Hayley." I began ticking facts off on my fingers. "Number one, Jonathan is helping us. Number two, Flynn showed Derek that text. Number three, yesterday Flynn volunteered to get me a criminal attorney if, in the heat of the moment, mind you, I'd helped Betsy Bell kill Nathaniel."

"What!" Hayley said coming up off the bed and putting her hands on her hips. "Flynn can't think that Betsy Bell is a murderess. He was so good to her when she was having that fight with Alexandra. Then he held down the fort at her tent while y'all went to talk to the attorney. Sold over a thousand dollars' worth of Betsy Bell's Regency dresses."

"Be that as it may, Flynn offered me an attorney in case I'd helped Betsy Bell kill him. Course, he backed down when I said that he could very well be the killer. None of us really knows him. He's not from here. And listen to this: last night Detective Gordon came up to my table at Gator's. He was trying to get me to comment on Betsy Bell's temper. I wouldn't, but guess what he said."

"No idea."

"He told me that Nathaniel had stolen Flynn's girlfriend in Williamsburg," I said triumphantly. "I can't wait to ask Flynn about it. Gives him a motive for murder, don't you think?"

Hayley sighed. "No. I can't see it."

"What? I thought you weren't particularly fond of Flynn since he showed that text to Derek."

"True. I was annoyed with him for not deleting your text and for showing it to Derek. But I realized he had no choice in the matter. As for him wanting to get you an attorney, that could be seen as protective."

I snorted. "Most of the time, I don't think he even likes me."

"I don't know about that. Flynn's eyes are on you when you're not looking."

"Well, if he thinks I'm a murderer, maybe he's watching my every move, guarding his life," I said, my sarcasm level sitting on ten.

"Talk sense, Kay. I do want to hear what Flynn says about this alleged girlfriend that Nathaniel stole from him. Flynn is so good looking, especially compared to Nathaniel, all I can say is that girl hasn't got the sense God gave a duck. But Flynn's not a murderer. He's too much of a...a...well, gentleman I think is the word I'm searching for."

I crossed my arms. "Flynn doesn't like anything with sugar in it. And he's not much fun. Last night, Jonathan and I played a game of darts. It was great fun."

"I assume you won."

"Naturally. But I confess, I do like Jonathan."

"But we barely know him. Do you think we should believe what he says?"

I raised one shoulder in a half-shrug. "I don't see why not. We have the security video that proves what he says to be true."

We were quiet for a moment, then I said, "Hayley, I'm not looking for a boyfriend in the middle of a murder investigation. I don't know if I've gotten over what Warner did to me."

"Warner was a real piece of work breaking up with you when you thought he was going to ask you to marry him. Just like the Warner in Legally Blonde did to Elle Woods. You know, I've often wondered if that's where your Warner got the idea to take you out to dinner and dump you."

"I did watch the movie with him."

"Uh-huh. Plus, I'll never know what Warner saw in living in New York City. When I went to culinary school there, the place made my anxiety go through the roof. I couldn't handle it."

"Warner was determined to leave Boring and all of us."

"Funny. Flynn has lived in London and yet he chose to settle in Virginia."

"We don't know if he's staying in Jane Austen Town or going back to Colonial Williamsburg or somewhere else. I asked him, and he didn't answer."

"That's the trouble with living in a small town. Some men can't appreciate a close community and feel they're missing out by not being in a big city. But I don't think Flynn will leave. Just a hunch."

"Oh wait! I haven't told you what Jonathan did for us," I said.

"Us?"

I nodded. "For the investigation. I told him that Nathaniel had been married, and we wanted to know who his wife was."

Hayley sat down on the edge of the bed. "How would he know who she was?"

"He didn't. But even though he said Silas Dale would fire him if he found out he'd done so, Jonathan used the casino's resources for background checks to find out. It's Sharon. Sharon Calhoun. Or I should say, Sharon Calhoun Grant."

"Get out of town!" Hayley exclaimed in disbelief.

"I was as shocked as you are. We have to talk to her," I said.

Hayley pulled out her cell phone and checked the time. "Sharon will be setting up at my tent in an hour. We'll catch her then."

At that moment, Aunt Adeline came into the room bearing a cup of tea for me. "Have either of y'all seen Cho? Kay, are the shades of Jane Austen Town to be thus polluted now that you're seeing Jonathan Warren? By the way, Flynn is downstairs eating my biscuits. He probably thinks they're scones. Anyway, he's waiting for you, Kay."

Chapter Thirteen

I showered and then, with Hayley and Aunt Adeline's help, dressed in a cream-colored Regency gown that had a dark green ribbon circling the high waist and green leaves embroidering the hem, the neckline, and the short sleeves. The dress came with a high-crowned bonnet decorated with felt leaves at the side and dark green ribbon that tied under my chin.

Aunt Adeline took Cho back to her suite. When she returned, I told her about Jonathan, his personal life, and how he didn't really like Silas Dale. I finished with how he'd helped by finding out who had been Nathaniel's wife.

"Gracious! I didn't make the connection, it's been so long ago," Aunt Adeline said. "I recall Ida being tore up when Sharon got married. Sharon was only nineteen. He took her to Vegas for the wedding. So tacky."

"That wouldn't have gone down well with Mrs. Calhoun," I said.

Aunt Adeline shook her head. "It didn't. Add that to the fact that Ida thought Sharon's new husband was too big for his britches and would never amount to a hill of beans and the subject was pretty much off limits between us. Ida's instincts were correct. Not long after Sharon had Palmer, they got a divorce."

"Twenty years ago?" Hayley asked.

"That'd be about right," Aunt Adeline agreed. "But for him to be murdered! If that don't take the biscuit."

Speaking of biscuits, as we reached the kitchen, I saw Flynn sitting by himself, eating Aunt Adeline's biscuits and scrolling through his phone. As we entered, he rose. He wore a bottle-green Regency coat and tan colored breeches tucked into boots. His cravat was a work of art. I felt lightheaded.

Just breathe, Kay.

He said, "Good morning, ladies. Adeline, these rolls, erm, I mean biscuits are different than the ones I've had in England, but they're delicious."

"Thank you, Flynn," Aunt Adeline said. "I'm pleased you like them."

We all sat down. I filled my plate with two biscuits, some margarine, and a glob of strawberry jam. Reaching for the coffee pot, I said, "Flynn, you should relax your no sugar rule just this once. Those biscuits would be even better if you put some honey or jam on them."

Flynn gave me a chilly look but his tone was light. "Do you always judge people by their food choices or just me?"

I drew in a breath, but Hayley saved me from saying something I might regret. "Kay, how many times have I told you that margarine is no substitute for butter?"

"I know, but I haven't been doing my daily run so I have to make at least a token gesture to the state of my waistline."

"Something you must have forgotten when you chose a dining establishment last night," Flynn said and stirred his tea efficiently without the spoon hitting the insides of the china teacup.

I put a big spoonful of sugar in my coffee and stirred it noisily. "At least my supper companion did everything he could to help me with the investigation rather than offer me an attorney in case I'd committed the crime."

"Ooooh, burn," Hayley said under her breath.

"I was merely trying to protect you," Flynn said.

"Oh, was that it?" I said innocently. Then, "Turns out Sharon Calhoun was Nathaniel's ex-wife."

"How did Jonathan Warren know that?" Flynn asked, frozen in place.

"He risked his job to help me by using the casino resort's background check system to find out about Nathaniel Grant. Impressive, no?"

"It's interesting, I'll say. First, he tries to destroy the town, now he's helping us. I wonder what's motivating him."

"I think he has a crush on Kay," Aunt Adeline said. "I noticed it back in September when Jonathan came down with Silas Dale."

"Really?" Flynn said.

He had a crease between his eyes as if he couldn't figure out why anyone would think me attractive.

"We must speak with Sharon immediately," he said.

"She'll be setting up food in my tent in a few minutes," Hayley said. "We'll all go."

"Ida will be coming here any minute," Aunt Adeline said. "She's baking shortbread, rout-cakes, and a rum cake for my card party tonight. Then we're putting together finger sandwiches."

"That sounds delicious," Hayley said. "I've never tried making rout-cakes."

"Ida hasn't made them before, but I'm sure they'll turn out good," Aunt Adeline mused, her mind on something else. "I suppose I should talk to Ida about Nathaniel and Sharon. After all, Ida did tell me about the marriage. I'd just forgotten the groom's name."

"Only if you're comfortable doing so," I said.

Aunt Adeline nodded. "I'll find a way that won't hurt her feelings or damage our friendship."

We finished eating, then Hayley and I put on spencer jackets, pulled on our white gloves and, with Flynn's escort, we headed off for Hayley's Bakery tent.

But when we got there, it was to find Valeria on her own. She had her phone in her hand and she jumped when she saw us.

"Where's Sharon?" Hayley asked her. "Why are you so nervous?"

"I was just going to call you. Detective Gordon and Officer Fowler took Sharon away in their police car." Valeria's voice clogged with tears.

Flynn said, "So, I expect they took her to the police station."

"They did not say so, but I think that's where they went. Why would they want to grill Sharon? I don't think she knew the man that was murdered."

"Maybe it's about something else, something she might have seen," I said trying to soothe Valeria.

"It's possible, but I don't have a good feeling about this," Valeria said shaking her head in the negative. "Sharon's face went white, like she'd seen a ghost."

The ghost of her dead ex-husband.

Hayley looked at me. "I need to stay here and help Valeria get set up for the day. I might text Percy and see if he can help. The festival will open in less than an hour. I'll let you know if Sharon comes back."

"Okay, I want to talk to Alexandra in the meantime. I'll see if I can catch her at the Farmhouse Inn."

"I'll go with you," Flynn said.

"Fine," I replied. No use arguing with him.

As we walked toward the Farmhouse Inn, I thought about how, while I'd told Hayley what Detective Gordon had said about Nathaniel stealing Flynn's girlfriend, I hadn't told Aunt Adeline. I didn't know why I hadn't, and it bothered me.

The sun shone above taking the chill off the morning. I looked up at one of the pole banners that depicted Jane Austen's image and wondered what she'd think of all this. Townsfolk and out of town vendors were pushing tent flaps aside, getting ready for the new day. Mayor Buckalew walked around gladhanding everyone with a big smile on his face like there wasn't an ongoing murder investigation. He carried a box of Buster's Big Size Pies and handed them out.

Lorraine Longo greeted me as she walked by. "Morning, Flynn. Kay, good to see you alive and well this morning after your night out at Gator's," she said with a wink.

"I'm perfectly fine," I called after her.

"Lorraine must have seen you with Jonathan Warren last night," Flynn said.

"She did. She was just teasing me," I said.

"Hmm."

My brother, Neil, strode toward us, a camera suspended from a thick strap around his neck.

"Good morning, Kay, Flynn. Can I get a photo of you two dressed in your Regency finery for the *Jane Austen Town Gazette*?"

I hesitated, then said, "Sure."

Flynn moved in close to me and put his arm lightly around my waist. We smiled for the camera and then Flynn stepped away.

At his warm touch, the scene around me faded out and then came back in focus.

Get ahold of yourself, Kay.

Flynn was saying, "Neil, I thought it quite clever how you did Headlines From 1811 on the *Gazette's* website."

"Thanks. I've got an old-fashioned paper newspaper version that should be here by noon. I want them for sale this afternoon. Any news on the investigation?"

"None for print," I said with a smile.

Neil raised his arms in surrender. "Off the record."

"We're going to the Farmhouse Inn to talk with Alexandra Bartholomew," Flynn said. "She was romantically involved with Nathaniel Grant. She said as much during an argument she had with Betsy Bell in front of us."

Neil nodded. "I heard about that. But you won't find Alexandra at the Farmhouse Inn. I saw her in Monday's Country Store a few minutes ago looking at hair products. Betsy Bell Ward was further down the aisle. Those two ladies looked like they were about to butt heads so I chatted with Alexandra until Betsy Bell left."

"Good thinking, Neil," Flynn said. "What did Betsy Bell buy?"

Neil grimaced. "Disposable gloves."

"Don't look like that, Neil," I said. "She could be using those for any number of things. Excuse us. We have to catch up to Alexandra."

Flynn walked alongside me as we wound our way through the tents in the direction of Monday's Country Store.

Alexandra had just come down the steps of the store when we spotted her. She had on a skintight pair of jeans, knee-high, heeled black boots, and a one-shoulder fuzzy black sweater. She wasn't carrying a package. I assumed none of the hair products had been good enough for her. As we approached, her expression turned wary.

Flynn smiled at her and Alexandra's face immediately relaxed.

He said, "Alexandra, would you be good enough to help us with a few questions?"

She ignored me and looked Flynn up and down. "I'll always answer a question put to me by a handsome gentleman."

I could smell her Dior perfume and saw she was overly made-up again.

"May I get you something to drink?" he asked her.

"It's a little early for me. Ask again at noon," she said with a flirtatious grin.

Flynn turned to me. "Kay?"

"No, thank you."

"Shall we sit at one of the picnic tables?" he asked. He led the way and Alexandra sat next to him while I sat across from them.

"We're hoping you can tell us more about Nathaniel Grant, Alexandra."

"You're trying to find out who killed him," Alexandra said flatly.

"Yes," I said.

She looked startled to see me sitting there. I decided to let Flynn run with the questions. Alexandra would respond more freely with him.

She smoothed a hand over her perfect hair. "Obviously Betsy Bell did it."

"Why do you say that?" Flynn asked.

She snorted. "Are you kidding? I heard she was found over his dead body holding a pair of scissors from her store. They were dripping with Nathaniel's blood. Anyone with a brain in their head knows she killed him."

"What would be her motive?" Flynn asked.

"Jealousy. You heard her when she attacked me over him. She wanted him for herself and couldn't stand the fact that he was with me. The woman may sound sweet and innocent, but she only fools the local yokels. She's a cold-blooded murderer."

I bit my tongue at the "local yokels" comment and clenched my fists in my lap.

"You knew him well, then?" Flynn asked.

"Of course. Nathaniel worked for me at my bed and breakfast, Bartholomew's, in Massachusetts. I hold immersive Jane Austen weekends. Well attended, I might add, with a chef from Boston preparing meals. I heard of Nathaniel's reputation and hired him to teach English Country Dances to my guests."

So she lied to the police saying Nathaniel merely worked for her.

"Did he work for you once or more often?" Flynn asked.

"Oh, by the third weekend we were talking about becoming partners in my business and well, in life," she said.

As if Nathaniel would give up other women for her.

"What made you come to Jane Austen Town?" Flynn asked.

She chuckled. "Sort of a busman's holiday. I thought perhaps I'd pick up Jane Austen ideas that I could implement with more grace at Bartholomew's. And, Nathaniel was going to be working here. He begged me to come down."

He so did not. This woman and the truth weren't related. And we were plenty graceful in Jane Austen Town! Don't say anything, Kay.

"When was the last time you saw him?" Flynn asked sympathetically.

"We had a cozy late supper last Tuesday. I'll always remember it. Nathaniel was so tender with me. Then I came to his dance class on Thursday to be supportive."

"I'm sorry for your loss." Flynn gave her a gentle smile. "Did you pick up any ideas for your B & B?"

"From this little festival? No indeed. I did create a scheme of my own though that I can't wait to implement. It will be based on the main character in *Sense & Sensibility* who was a matchmaker. A matchmaking weekend! Doesn't that sound entertaining?"

That does it.

"What were you and Nathaniel arguing about at the dance class?" I asked.

She looked down her nose at me with a frigid glare. "I beg your pardon?"

"I was there. You were angry and hissed something in his ear before you left the class. He laughed at you."

She waved a careless hand. "I don't even remember. Whatever it was, it didn't mean anything. A lover's quarrel."

"Really? Because twenty minutes later when I returned to the Assembly Rooms and found Nathaniel Grant dead, your J'Adore perfume almost knocked me over when I walked into the room. Did you come back to talk to him more about your 'lover's quarrel'?"

She narrowed her eyes at me. "You must have been the one that put that thought into Detective Gordon's head. He put the same question to me. I'll tell you what I told him: I did not return to the building. I had no reason to kill Nathaniel. We were planning our future together. I'll miss him dreadfully."

Flynn said, "You needed him for your business. Your B & B hasn't been profitable, has it? More of a vanity project for you, I expect."

Wow! Where did Flynn get that intel? Not just a handsome face, was he.

"I've already said that we were planning to become business partners," Alexandra said and stood as if to leave.

Something Hugo had said came to me. "Nathaniel wasn't going to move to Massachusetts to be with you, though, was he? Too cold up there for someone who loves year-round beaches and lots of bikini-clad women. Is that what he told you that made you angry? What did you do? Sneak back into the Assembly Rooms and argue with him without getting anywhere? Did you see the scissors on the table, pick them up and—"

"Silence!" she yelled, her green eyes glittering with rage. She dashed around to my side of the picnic table.

I stood and so did Flynn.

She leaned in and spoke right in my face. "I'm warning you, Kay Starling. You'd better concentrate on your silly little festival and leave me alone. Stop making up stories about me or I promise you, I'll make you sorry!"

She marched away, blonde hair swinging, fury in every step.

Flynn came around the table. "I don't like the way she threatened you, Kay. What set you off like that? I was leading her into questions about the day Nathaniel was killed."

"She's a fake! She doesn't know anything about Jane Austen's work. The matchmaking heroine is Emma Woodhouse in the novel *Emma*. Nothing to do with *Sense and Sensibility*. That's a huge mistake to make and tells me everything I need to know about someone holding 'immersive' Jane Austen weekends. Alexandra is a liar. She's lying about Nathaniel wanting to be with her, too. As far as I'm concerned, she's moved to the top of my suspect list."

"Well done, Kay. I missed that clue."

I studied him. "That's understandable though, isn't it? You haven't read all of Jane Austen's books or seen any of the adaptations, have you?"

"Before I answer, I want to know what the punishment is for not being a Janeite whilst at the same time caring about the town and the festival."

He looked into my eyes as he spoke.

"I never said you had to be a Janeite."

"According to your niece, Sarah Beth, I would have to read all the books and see all the adaptations in order to be considered a Janeite. I confess I haven't done either. But I admire Austen's body of work and how it's remained popular through many generations."

"Well, that's a start."

"I do know the story of *Pride and Prejudice*. We read it in school."

"Oh?"

"Yes," he said. He stepped back and adopted the posture of one on the stage addressing an audience. "You see, a very rich guy asks a lady with fine eyes to marry him, but she says she will not. Er, for some reason."

I couldn't help but smile at the dramatic way he told the story.

"Later, much later, she is out and about in the countryside and what does she see but his enormous estate with a huge house! Then she says she'll marry him."

He grinned at me.

I started laughing. Then I said, "Referencing the 1995 adaptation, I must tell you that you've left out the part where she sees him coming back to his house after a swim."

He gave me a mock puzzled look. "Why does that matter?"

"Never mind!"

"It matters because his shirt is wet. That's the reason why the 1995 version is the favorite amongst ladies everywhere." His eyes twinkled.

"No," I said setting aside the mental image of the poster of Colin Firth emerging from the lake that was on my bedroom wall. "The 1995 version is a favorite because it's the most faithful to the novel."

"Right, I—" he stopped abruptly, his manner turning serious. "It's Sharon. She's coming this way."

Chapter Fourteen

I t didn't take much to convince Sharon to agree to come to the Golden Age Diner with us. She'd been on her way to Monday's Country Store to pick up a drink and a snack. She wanted to take a little time to compose herself before returning to Hayley's Bakery tent and facing friends and the public.

Valeria had been right: Sharon's face was milk white. Her hand trembled as she reached for the coffee that Francie had brought her.

Flynn and I sat across from her in the booth.

"I can't imagine getting married when I was nineteen," I said to break the ice. "At that age, I'd barely dated. It was all I could do to concentrate on my college studies."

"Nate swept me off my feet," Sharon said, her eyes fixed on the tabletop. "He treated me so well, leaving little presents for me on my doorstep, telling me I was the queen of his world. He had such big plans for the future, our future. Nate acted like it was a forgone conclusion that we would marry."

"Where did you meet him?" Flynn asked.

"At a dance at the community center. It was the first really warm night in May that year. The dance was crowded. Nate was the best dancer in the room, impressing all the girls. But after he danced with me, he didn't dance with another girl the rest of the night. I felt special."

She paused and took a sip of her coffee. I noticed how she called Nathaniel "Nate," something Flynn told me not to do. I wondered if the nickname reminded Nathaniel of this time in his life.

"From that night on, we were inseparable. Mama didn't like him, but I thought she was just being old-fashioned. Plus, I think Nate's free spirit reminded her of my daddy. He took off when I was seven. Now that I look back on it, I think Mama was worried about any child of mine suffering the same fate."

Sharon took off her knitted headband and rubbed the wool between her fingers before dropping it in her lap. "When I told Nate I was pregnant, he seemed pleased. He said he had money saved and we could go to Vegas and get married. The bride's supposed to pay for the wedding, but I was flipping burgers in Harrisonburg at the time and hadn't saved any money. When I told Mama I was getting married, she hit the roof. But off I went to Vegas with Nate. Six months later, I had Palmer."

For the first time, Sharon's face softened.

"He's in medical school over in Richmond, isn't he?" I asked.

She looked at me. "He is. He's a fine boy, well, a man now. The best thing that ever happened to me. Back when Palmer was born, Nate acted like the proud father, handing out those cigars made of chewing gum. But he couldn't handle being an actual father, hated it when Palmer cried, hated paying for Palmer's car seat and pediatrician appointments. I had put on some weight, too, and Nate didn't like that either. Palmer wasn't even walking yet when Nate left. He'd gotten involved with ballroom dancing and got a job down in Florida. He wasn't interested in family life. He certainly wasn't interested in helping me financially with taking care of Palmer."

"He didn't send funds for his child?" Flynn asked.

Sharon shook her head, her gaze back on the tabletop. "No. He told me that I'd have to take him to court and a judge would have to threaten to throw him in jail before he'd give me a dime. I did get a court order for child support, but Nate ignored it. I couldn't afford an attorney to fight him."

"What about seeing Palmer?" I asked, livid that the man had treated his own child this way.

"Nate came back to Virginia on Palmer's second birthday, arms full of presents. Palmer didn't know who he was. That was the last time Nate saw Palmer. Or me. I think he was ashamed of us, living out in the trailer, you know. Country people. Whereas he saw himself as not just a dancing instructor, but an entertainer. Had that YouTube channel and all."

"I am so sorry, Sharon," I said.

"Don't be. I chose him. It was my decision to marry him. It's my fault that Palmer grew up without a father." She burst into tears.

Flynn reached into his pocket and pulled out a linen handkerchief and handed it to her. "That was Nathaniel's choice, not yours. Had I known he was such a tosser, I would never have considered bringing him here, Sharon. I apologize."

She wiped her face with the handkerchief, then said, "When I found out Nate was in town, my first thought was that I would avoid him at all costs. I was happy that Palmer was away in Richmond so his father couldn't upset him. Then, I couldn't stop thinking about how sweet it would be to tell Nate off. Tell him how he lost out on a great son. You know, growing up poor has different effects on people. On Palmer, he looked around him and wanted to help. He sees being a doctor in a rural area as a way to do that."

"What did you decide to do?" I asked, holding my breath. I didn't want Sharon to say she'd seen him, or worse, she'd killed him in the heat of the moment.

"I came to town for groceries. I knew Nate was at the community center where we'd met all those years ago. I found myself walking over there, almost in a dream."

She started trembling. I feared she was going to confess. I looked at Flynn. His eyes were on Sharon. He had one hand resting on the table. It was clenched into a fist.

Francie approached. I shook my head at her and she turned in the other direction.

In a low voice, Sharon said, "I walked up the steps to where the dance lessons were supposed to be held. I remember smelling perfume. Then I was in the doorway, and Nate was laying on the floor, something in his back. I couldn't really see what it was, but he wasn't moving. I saw the blood across his shirt. I turned and ran back down the stairs and outside. I was terrified."

I exhaled a breath I hadn't realized I'd been holding.

"Did you see anyone when you exited the building?" Flynn asked.

Sharon took a sip of her cold coffee. "There were people around, but I was concentrating on looking normal. I couldn't tell you who they were. My mind was racing. All I could think was that if Nate had been murdered, the police would think I did it. It's always the spouse or the ex-spouse on TV shows and movies, right?"

I smiled at her. "Yes. Try to think, though, Sharon. You didn't recognize anyone outside? Someone else going into the building, or hurrying down the street?"

She shook her head. "No. It was like a thick fog had been dropped on my world. I'd left my car at Starling's Grocery. I went back there and made myself go in the store, pick up the items on my list, and get in the car. By then, I'd stopped shaking and could drive home."

"Did you tell any of this to Detective Gordon this morning?" Flynn asked.

"No. I kept telling him that I hadn't talked to Nate in years. Which is true." Sharon fidgeted with Flynn's handkerchief. "I don't know what to do if Detective Gordon finds out I was there. Are either of you going to tell him? I know you're trying to help Betsy Bell."

Flynn sat with a stony expression.

I didn't want to say whether or not I'd be speaking to Detective Gordon. The truth was, I didn't want to get Sharon into more trouble until I'd had a chance to think. "Sharon, do you have any idea who might have killed Nate?"

She drew in a breath. "I've thought about it a lot. Since I hadn't seen or spoken to him in so long, I don't know who was in his life that would have hated him enough to commit murder. I have heard gossip about Nate and that woman from up north, Alexandra. When I passed by her at the festival, I smelled the exact same perfume as I smelled when I was going up the steps at the community center. But that might not mean anything. Or maybe it could."

I'd say it meant we'd found our killer.

Sharon picked up her headband and put it back on.

"Pretty," I said, indicating the headband.

"Thanks. I'm a Yarnie. Love to knit. I started back when Palmer was a toddler. Something to help the stress. Look, if y'all don't have any more questions, I should get over to Hayley's tent. I've left them without help for long enough."

"You won't stay and have lunch?" Flynn asked.

She shook her head. "No, thank you, Flynn. Kay, if I think of anything else, I'll text you, okay? And if you need me or hear anything more about Alexandra, you let me know. If I can help, I will. It's a whole lot easier talking to you than Detective Gordon."

When she stood to go, I rose and gave her a light hug. She was stiff in my arms at first, then she hugged me hard before making her way out of the diner.

I sat down. "I want to believe her. I will say it's a good thing Nate, which is what I'm calling him now, is already dead."

"I expect there's a line of people who wanted to kill him," Flynn said.

I debated with myself for a moment, then said, "You sure you weren't one of them? I heard something about a girlfriend of yours preferring Nate."

He looked confused for a second. Then, "Maddy. Remember the woman in Colonial Williamsburg who I spoke to over the phone about Nathaniel?"

"Yes."

"She and I had dinner twice. Then Nathaniel came on the scene and she started going out with him. That didn't last long either. She's got her cardiologist fiancé now. How did you know?"

"Last night, when I was with Jonathan at Gator's, Detective Gordon mentioned it."

"He hasn't said anything to me about it and I'm not volunteering any more information," he said and then paused for moment. "I see no reason to rush to him with this information from Sharon either. I want to believe her."

Kind. He really is very kind. But then, so is Jonathan.

"I think Alexandra killed Nate."

"Possibly," he said.

"Definitely. I think Nate was finished with her. That gives her motive. She was at the Assembly Rooms. There's opportunity especially with Betsy Bell's scissors conveniently on the table."

"How could we find out if fingerprints were on the scissors?"

I shook my head. "Detective Gordon isn't going to tell us. That's if he even has the results back yet from Harrisonburg. Maybe we should just tell him what we've found out about Alexandra."

"Would he believe us? We've no hard evidence."

I sighed. "Maybe not."

"Let's consider it further after we've had lunch. Do you have time before giving the archery lessons? I'd wager they have cupcakes here. I know how much you like them." He signaled Francie.

Maddening man!

Miss June came to our table with menus.

"How are you, Miss June?" Flynn asked.

"Tolerable fair. I see you got around to questioning the wife."

"You knew Sharon was married to Nathaniel?" I exclaimed.

"Course I did! I wasn't born yesterday! I remember the whole thing, Sharon meetin' him, them running off to Vegas when she was supposed to be registering for community college. Ida Calhoun could have skinned him alive. For all I know, when he showed up here again, she did. He was trash. And trash needs taking out."

Chapter Fifteen

"Thank you, Miss Starling. It was fun!"

"I don't know if archery is for me," a woman groaned.

"Enjoyed this so much! I need my own bow and arrow!"

As the last of the students left my archery class, I walked across the grass in Dogwood Park to the archery target. I needed to dismantle it and gather up all the equipment. The sound of hoofbeats caught my attention.

"Hey, sis. You need help?" Hugo called.

Holding a hand to my brow to shade my eyes from the fading afternoon sun, I saw Hugo, Bowie, and Percy alighting from Hugo's carriage. Bowie took off running around the duck pond.

"Hey y'all. I could use a hand," I answered. I rubbed my right forearm and winced.

"Didn't wear an arm guard, did you, Kay?" Hugo said and frowned.

"Forgot."

"Your left eye must be dominant," Percy said. "Is that why you're shooting left-handed?"

"Yes, I've always shot that way."

"That bowstring will slap your forearm when you shoot," Percy said. "Was your grip too tight?"

I nodded. "I think it was. My feet were here but my mind was on this murder investigation."

"Anything new?" Hugo asked, tilting his top hat back.

"Alexandra Bartholomew is at the top of my suspect list, but I'll have to talk to y'all later. I need to put all this equipment away so I can go to Candice Hern's talk. She's doing her 'What a Lady Carried in Her Reticule in the Time of Jane Austen.' I hear it's not to be missed."

"From the way the Park is emptying out, I'd say that's true," Hugo said.

"We'll help you so you can go," Percy said.

"After the carriage is loaded up, we'll take everything down to the storage shed," Hugo said.

We all worked together until the archery equipment was tucked in the carriage. Hugo whistled for Bowie. "We'll talk later, Kay. I want to know about your evening at Gator's," he said. His tone of voice was even but he had a dubious look on his face that brothers worldwide have perfected.

"Okay."

He walked away. The set of his shoulders told me he was anxious on my account. Wait until he heard about how Flynn and I had questioned not only Alexandra, but Sharon.

Percy lagged behind. "Kay, I've been trying to get ahold of Hayley but she hasn't answered my calls or texts."

"She's busy with this festival, Percy. I can tell her you asked after her if you'd like."

"Please do. Thank you."

I watched as he joined Hugo and Bowie and they drove away.

I started walking to the parking lot, but stopped and pulled out my phone. I texted Flynn.

Finished archery lesson. Going to the Candice Hern talk in the church hall.

The three dots appeared, so I waited for his response. Maybe he had something lined up about the investigation.

Right. Helping Adeline and Ida prepare for the card party later. We just finished making rum cake.

How much rum have you had?

None. I rarely drink alcohol. Setting up the card tables and chairs. See you later?

Maybe.

Heading across the grass I found myself smiling for no reason when I heard cawing above me. A crow circled above. "Henry Tilney, is that you?"

"Caw! Caw!" he cried and swooped down.

He was after my bonnet again, that mischievous bird. "Stop that right now!" I shouted.

Everything happened at once.

Tilney swooped over me again.

I ducked but tripped, lost my balance, and fell to the ground on my knees.

I heard a "Whoosh!" close to me.

Saw the arrow. Felt the pain. Everything went black.

***

The first thing I heard when I came to was a beeping sound. Then something was pulled across my chest and there was a click. The beeping stopped. Searing pain emanated from my right forearm. Was it the from the bowstring? No, the arrow. I came fully awake just as driver's side door opened.

"Jonathan? What happened?"

"Kay! Thank God, you're conscious. Someone shot you with an arrow. I'm taking you to the hospital. I've called ahead. They're expecting us."

I struggled to sit up and failed. He'd put my seat back and laid me down. Pain made my mind foggy. I heard the GPS lady say, "Turn left on Dogwood Park Drive."

"I don't need a hospital. It's just my arm."

Had someone tried to kill me? If Tilney had not dive-bombed me causing me to fall, would the arrow have hit my chest?

"No, ma'am, there'll be no arguing. Hush and let me concentrate on the directions. We'll be there in five minutes at most," Jonathan said in a tone that meant he wouldn't be discussing the matter further.

At Blue Ridge Community Hospital, the emergency room doctor, Dr. Fannon, was young and compassionate making me think of how Sharon's son, Palmer, might be once he got his degree. Dr. Fannon examined me while making me go over exactly what had happened. He ordered an MRI of my right arm and said he'd be back.

My nurse, Keisha, had taken off my spencer jacket which I noticed had blood down one sleeve. My bare arm revealed redness and a bruise coming up from the bowstring injury near my elbow. But down my forearm there was a lump the size of a ping pong ball which the doctor had said was a hematoma with a cut inside. Keisha efficiently cleaned it, then wrapped it to stop the bleeding.

"On a scale of one to ten with ten being the worst pain you've ever felt, how bad is your pain?" Keisha asked.

I tensed. "Eight, maybe a nine," I squeaked.

"I'll see what I can give you," she said and hurried out.

There was a curtain dividing me from the other patients. Jonathan had stood back respectfully while the doctor examined me. Now, he came to my bedside. "This is terrible, Kay. I told you to leave the murder investigation to the police. If you hadn't fallen, I hate to think where that arrow would have struck you."

I noticed spots and lines of blood on his pale blue shirt. My blood from when he'd carried me to his car. I shivered.

Keisha came back with a little clear cup containing two pills. She handed me a cup of water so I could swallow it. When I'd done so, I asked, "What was it?"

"Extra strength Tylenol. I'm putting this ice pack on you until they take you down to Radiology. Ice is your best friend when it comes to pain." She glanced from me to Jonathan. "You'll be staying and then taking her home, sir?"

"Yes, ma'am. I'm not going anywhere without her." He smiled, showing his dimples.

Keisha looked back at me. "When the doctor decides you can go home, you'll be receiving discharge instructions. You have a touch of shock so after you leave here tonight, it'll be best for you to stay in bed or sit and watch TV. No driving, be extra careful going up and down stairs."

I nodded wishing the Tylenol would kick in.

When the nurse left, Jonathan came to my side again. The dimples were gone. He frowned at me. "I wanted to see you today, but I'm not sure of my welcome around here and wanted to minimize my interference. I have a festival program booklet and saw you were giving the archery lessons. I thought maybe Dogwood Park would be a good place for us to talk."

"I'm really glad you came."

"So am I, Kay," he said, taking my left hand and holding it. "I saw the person that shot you with the arrow."

"Who was it?" My right arm might have felt like it had been through a wood chipper but my left suddenly felt warm and cozy.

He shook his head. "I couldn't tell. She was wearing a hoodie and standing with her back to me by that big oak tree about fifteen yards from where you were."

"She?"

He looked away, a crease forming between his eyes. I could tell he was trying to see the scene again in his mind.

He faced me. "I thought it was a woman, but I reckon it could have been a man. I shouted when I saw the person draw back the bow and I realized their intention. But I was too late. They ran off after firing that arrow at you. I thought it was much more important that I see to you than go after them."

Right then, a tall, dark-skinned guy whose nametag read "Breon" came around the curtain with a wheelchair causing Jonathan to release my hand. "You Kay Starling?"

"Yes."

"If you can tell me your correct date of birth," he said in the tone of a game show host, "I'll take you down to meet The Big Donut."

I did, then he and Jonathan helped me into the wheelchair.

After the MRI, I was wheeled back to the curtained off area where Jonathan sat in a chair waiting for me. I noticed once again how boyishly handsome he was although right now, worry clouded his expression.

The pain medicine had kicked in, thankfully, but I was thirsty. I looked for my water.

"You want a Coke?" Jonathan asked.

"Sure."

"What kind?"

I hesitated for a second then realized he meant what kind of soda did I want. "A diet Coke would be great."

"Diet? Surely, you're not worried about your figure. You're beautiful. Why not a regular Coke? The calories would probably do you good right now."

"Thank you. A regular Coke it is," I said, thinking how thoughtful he was. "Wait, Jonathan. Are you going to tell Silas Dale about this?"

"About your liking Coke when he drinks Dr. Pepper? Nah," he said and winked in a conspiratorial manner.

When he came back with a plastic cup full of ice and the can of Coke, he opened it and poured it for me. "Here. Should you let someone know where you are?"

I had been savoring the cold drink and almost choked. "Mercy! Where's my phone? I need to text my aunt."

But Dr. Fannon returned with Keisha at that moment preventing me from doing so.

"Miss Starling, you're in luck," Dr. Fannon said with a smile. "There are two forearm bones: the ulna and the radius. Both of yours are fine. You do have a cut in that hematoma and likely some muscle bruising, so you'll need to wear a sling."

The nurse arranged my bad arm in the sling while he spoke.

"Ice for twenty minutes at a time as often as you can for the first twenty-four hours. Take two extra strength Tylenol every eight hours. I also want you to take a course of antibiotics. Which pharmacy do you use?"

"Mr. Bexley's Pharmacy on Main Street."

"Kay, it's after seven. Will they still be open?" Jonathan asked.

Dr. Fannon answered for me. "They won't be. How about I put in the order to the hospital pharmacy? You can pick it up before you go home."

"Thank you. That would be best," I told him and smiled at Jonathan.

"Okay, I hope you get to feeling better. Follow up with your primary care physician or come back here if the pain worsens or you see any sign of an infection. I'm discharging you, but before you go, someone's here to see you. Take care."

I'd barely taken in what he said when Officer Fowler came around the curtain. She flipped open a notebook and looked from me to Jonathan and back to me.

"This is Jonathan Warren," I said guardedly, remembering how Brock Winthrop had told me not to speak to the police without him.

"What's your address, Mr. Warren? I understand you're a witness to the incident."

He gave her his New Jersey address.

"Where are you staying here in Virginia?"

"At the Stay a While Inn over in Charlottesville."

"And what's your business in Boring?"

"Jane Austen Town," I corrected.

Jonathan said, "I'm here for the Jane Austen Festival."

"Mmm-hmm. It's turning out to be a lively event. What happened in the park, Miss Starling? I have here from the hospital that you 'Arrived at the ER with a wound inflicted by an arrow as stated by patient. Male accompanying patient claims someone shot the arrow at her deliberately.' Who shot you deliberately?"

"I don't know. Besides, I believe I told you and Detective Gordon that my attorney instructed me not to speak with you about the murder investigation without him."

She wrote notes as fast as she talked. I wondered if she knew shorthand. "So, this incident was related to Nathaniel Grant's death?"

"I'm on pain medicine and don't know what I'm saying," I told her.

She slid me a disbelieving look. "Probably gave you a couple of Tylenol." She looked at Jonathan. "Mr. Warren, did you see the person who shot an arrow at Miss Starling?"

"No ma'am, not exactly. I saw a person wearing a hoodie, with a bow and arrow, aim at Miss Starling. I saw the arrow hit her. I ran to help."

"You don't know who the person in the hoodie was?"

"No, ma'am."

"Did you see their face?"

"No, I never saw their face. Everything happened so fast."

"Miss Starling, have you been questioning people about Mr. Grant's death?"

I pressed my lips together.

Officer Fowler snapped her notebook closed and walked out without another word.

"Where were her manners?" Jonathan asked. "She didn't even say goodbye or wish you well."

We chuckled.

He handed me my reticule. "I'm assuming your phone is in this interesting purse."

"Thanks."

"I'm going to pick up your prescription, then bring the car around. Don't you dare move, you hear? I'm assuming they'll bring your discharge papers. Promise me you won't get out of the bed without help."

"Promise."

When he was gone, I retrieved my phone. Six missed calls. Nineteen missed texts. Aunt Adeline was worried sick. So was Hayley.

I quickly texted my aunt. *I'm as sorry as I can be. I am fine. Just some trouble at the park with my arm. At BRCH. Jonathan is bringing me home right now. Please don't worry. Love you.*

Chapter Sixteen

We rode back to Starling Farm in the quiet of Jonathan's Lincoln Aviator, a huge, luxurious vehicle. At the hospital, he'd helped me from the wheelchair into the passenger seat. It was odd to have gone into the hospital in the sunshine and come out in the dark.

"Your hat is ruined. It's in the back seat. Afraid you got blood on your pretty dress," he said.

"I hope there isn't any inside on the seats or door," I said, squinting in the darkness. The clock told me it was nearly eight.

"Don't give a second thought to that, Kay. I'm worried about you. What if this person tries to hurt you again?"

"I'm not holding any more archery lessons."

"I'm serious. Think about your safety. Try to always be with other people, preferably in a public place. Is that reticule thing big enough to carry a gun?"

"Yes, but I can't see myself shooting someone. You said the person who did it looked like a woman, right?"

"I believe it was. Can you think who it might be? Did you find Sharon Grant?"

"I've talked to her. They say you shouldn't rule anyone out, but I really don't think Sharon killed Nathaniel."

"Why?"

It was too complicated to answer. Besides, I could see the lights of home. I pointed with my left hand. "This is it. Turn here. It's a long driveway."

Jonathan navigated the drive. There were at least two dozen cars out front. Aunt Adeline's Regency card party must be in full swing. Jonathan parked as close as he could to the front door. He came around to my side of the car and opened the door.

"Come on, I've got you," he said, meaning to carry me.

"Maybe I can walk," I said. But when I tried, I felt dizzy and off balance from the weight of the sling which the nurse had packed with a giant disposable ice bag.

Without another word, he swept me into his arms and strode to the front door.

Aunt Adeline, Guthrie, Hayley, Hugo, and a scowling Flynn stood crowded together at the open door and met us before Jonathan could ring the doorbell.

"Hi everyone," I said. "This is Jonathan Warren."

"We know who he is," Flynn stated. "We met him when he and his boss tried to convert this town into a casino resort, remember?"

Aunt Adeline took control. "Good evening, Mr. Warren. Would you carry Kay up to her room? She looks like she needs her bed, and we're all anxious to hear what on earth happened."

"Yes, ma'am. It would be my pleasure," Jonathan said politely.

I thought I heard a low growl, but I didn't see Bowie. Then I saw the look on Hugo's face and knew where the growl had come from. I rolled my eyes at him.

Hayley had her arms crossed which was never a good sign.

Upstairs, Aunt Adeline led the way into my room. "If you'll put her down near her bathroom door, Mr. Warren, I'd be grateful. I'm sure Kay will want to change clothes. Hayley, bring one of Kay's Regency nightgowns and her blue velvet dressing gown."

Hayley rushed to the closet.

"Yes, Mrs. Starling," Jonathan said. He set me on my feet gently. Still, I had to cling to Aunt Adeline's arm for a minute to steady myself. Hayley brought my clothes and Aunt Adeline, treating me like I was five, took me into the bathroom and helped me change. "Not a word," she said. "No use having to repeat yourself for the benefit of the others."

"I'm sorry I worried you."

"You seem to be in one piece and that's all that matters," she said. "I want to hear what happened, then I must return to my guests. Ida is downstairs fussing over them now."

With Hayley's help, I was soon sitting up in bed, propped up by three pillows. I immediately felt the chill in the room, and it wasn't coming from my ice pack. The freeze was directed at Jonathan. No one said a word to him. He looked uncomfortable in his blood-stained shirt, jeans, and boots. Like a naughty boy who the adults weren't speaking to.

Immediately, I made quick work of explaining what had happened at the park after Hugo left with the equipment, how

Jonathan had come to my rescue, what the doctor had said about my wound, and how Officer Fowler had stopped by. While everyone listened intently, they avoided looking at Jonathan even when I praised how he'd taken care of me at the hospital. I started to get embarrassed and a little angry on Jonathan's behalf.

Guthrie broke the silence. "Who would want to kill our Kay?" he asked. "It must be an outsider."

Aunt Adeline said, "Mr. Warren, I can't thank you enough for all you've done for Kay today. May I offer you something to drink? A bite to eat? I've got plenty of food prepared downstairs."

"No ma'am, but thank you. I'm staying over in Charlottesville and best get on the road."

"I'll see you downstairs," Aunt Adeline said, putting up no argument.

"Please, don't trouble yourself, Mrs. Starling. I remember the way out." He looked at me with his sheepish smile. "Kay, I hope it will be all right if I call you tomorrow to see how you are."

"Thank you, Jonathan. I'd like that," I said.

Guthrie's gaze went from Aunt Adeline to Jonathan. "I'll walk down with you, Jonathan. I have a game of whist calling my name."

There was a low mumble of "Good night" and "Thank you" as Jonathan left with Guthrie.

The second they were out of the room, I turned on everyone. "What is wrong with all y'all? Jonathan came to my rescue when I was passed out flat on the ground! He took me to the hospital, stayed with me, got my medicine, and then brought me home. Have you forgotten your manners?"

Flynn said, "Have you forgotten that he works for the man trying to destroy this town? Under the circumstances, I'd say we were civil to him."

"Flynn's right. I know you think he's helping us, but I don't trust him," Hugo said.

Hayley asked, "How are you feeling, Kay? Are you in pain?"

"No, it's more of a dull ache. This ice has really helped."

"Good because I'm not in the habit of fussing at people in pain." She sat next to me on the bed. "Do you see my left eye twitching? I feel it twitching. It's been twitching since time passed this afternoon and I didn't hear from you. I had no idea what was going on and couldn't leave my sales tent to go looking for you. What would I do if you went and got yourself killed, huh?" She burst into tears.

"Hayley, hon don't cry," I said.

Hugo came forward, took a tissue out of the box on my bedside table and handed it to Hayley.

She swung around and glared at him. "Why'd you leave her alone in that park?"

Hugo's eyes popped. "How was I supposed to know someone would take a shot at her? She said she was going to a talk on women's purses or something."

"You should have escorted her there!" Hayley exclaimed and then loudly blew her nose.

"It's not like Jane Austen Town is a high-crime area," Hugo protested.

"Oh no," Hayley drawled. "No murders, attempted murders..."

Aunt Adeline cleared her throat. "Hayley's right. This was an attempt on your life, Kay. The police will investigate an attempted murder. I'll put in a call to Brock and get legal advice."

"I want to know who did this," Hugo fumed. "I'm going over to the park at first light and looking around. I know that big oak tree where Mr. Jonathan Warren said the attacker was hiding. Maybe they left something behind."

"An excellent idea," Flynn said. "I'll go with you."

"I'm going in my sitting room to call Brock," Aunt Adeline said. "Then I need to tend to my guests. Oh, Flynn filled us in on your meeting with Alexandra and your talk with Sharon, Kay. I think Ida considered there was a possibility that Sharon could have killed Nathaniel. She tried to tell me this afternoon that *she* had gone to see Nathaniel."

"What? Mrs. Calhoun wouldn't kill anyone," I said. "And why would she, or Sharon for that matter, wait all these years if she wanted Nate dead?"

"I agree. But my point is that Ida had *doubts* about her daughter. It's not just instinct that tells me Ida didn't kill Nathaniel. I *know* she couldn't have because I remember that day very well. After our morning planning committee meeting, I came back to the house. Ida was here and we worked in the kitchen together until around two-thirty when I left with Guthrie to go get Cho from Olive. I'm Ida's alibi."

"She fibbed thinking Sharon might have killed her ex?" Hayley said incredulously. "Almost makes Sharon seem guilty if her own mother thought her capable."

"It's something to consider," Aunt Adeline said then left the room.

Hugo said, "Come on, Flynn. Let's leave the ladies to talk. We can go down to the kitchen and get something to eat. Now that I know Kay is safe, I'm starving. Besides, I want to hear more about your interview with Sharon."

Flynn produced a paper copy of the *Jane Austen Town Gazette* and placed it on the bed next to me without a word. He followed Hugo out the door without a backward glance.

"What did I tell you about choosing margarine over butter?" Hayley asked me.

"Jonathan is not margarine and I said I'm not looking for a boyfriend. I am, however, looking for a glass of water or something to take my antibiotic."

"I'll run down to the kitchen and get you a ginger ale. Are you hungry?"

I smiled. Hayley and I always liked to have ginger ale whenever we were sick. A holdover from when we were little, I supposed. "I could eat a plate."

She leaned over and gave me a gentle hug. "Back in a flash."

Later, after I'd polished off dainty tea sandwiches consisting of smoked salmon and capers, pimento cheese (oops, not historically accurate but oh so delish), cucumber and onion-flavored cream cheese, curried egg salad, and another concoction Austen wouldn't recognize, deviled ham, Hayley sat on the bed next to me. We each had mugs of hot Twining's Lady Grey tea and shortbread rounds.

While we'd been eating, I'd given her my thoughts on the interviews Flynn and I had done with Alexandra and Sharon ending with, "My money is on Alexandra being the murderer. She's in really good shape too. Strong enough to shoot an arrow at me."

"Yeah, maybe. If she did kill Nate—love that we're calling him that now—I don't think she planned it. But I could see where she'd be furious that he wouldn't fall in with her plans to move up north. She goes back to the Assembly Rooms to try to make him come around to her way of thinking, he scoffs at her, laughs, maybe walks away from her." Hayley rose from the bed and held one hand high in the air. "She sees the scissors, grabs them, and plunges them in his back." Here Hayley swung her arm down and struck the Jane Austen book themed quilt on the bed. "I have to get one of these quilts when Hannah has time to make one."

I laughed. "One minute you're Sarah Siddons committing murder on stage, the next you're pining after the quilt."

"Just one of my many talents," she said. "As for Sharon, she's kind of a reserved person. Hard to tell what she's capable of, if you ask me. Some people can hold a grudge for decades."

"True."

We thought a few minutes, then Hayley said, "On the other hand, after what you told me, I don't think Sharon's self-esteem is where it should be. She might have messed up by marrying Nate, but she did a great job raising her son. She's been a hard worker at my sales tent."

"Josie says Sharon was a great admin assistant."

"All that adds up to Sharon being a responsible person. Could she really have snapped after all these years? Or did she have a motive we don't know about?"

"I don't know. I keep remembering what Aunt Adeline said to me about how everyone is a suspect until we rule them out."

"Not Betsy Bell. Girl is sweeter than a bee that's spent the day in honeysuckle flowers."

"She's been working so hard during the festival. I think she's worried about money what with the bottling plant closing."

"Lemme tell you. Betsy Bell is raking it in with orders for her Regency dresses. She's sold out of all the ones she sewed in the months leading up to the festival and taking orders for more. She'll be okay."

"That's good to hear."

"Have we ruled out Flynn?" Hayley asked observing me closely. "That question makes you uncomfortable, doesn't it?"

I let out a breath. "I can't say I'm actively thinking of him as a murderer. And don't say anything about him being a possible boyfriend. I can't read him. Sometimes it seems like Flynn doesn't even like me. If only I had Jane Austen's deep understanding of human nature."

"We all want that. Austen was a genius. As for Flynn, what I've seen is the way Flynn's hands balled into fists when Adeline read out your text from the hospital. He wanted to go up there and check out what was happening for himself. We had to practically physically restrain him, telling him you'd said you were on your way home."

"He likes to know everything and he likes to be in charge. I know that much about him."

"Huh. Who else do I know like that?" she said, tilting her head and raising her eyebrows at me. "Maybe that's why the two of you have clashed: you're alike."

"We are not. I would never pass up a cupcake." I declared. "Come on now, Hayley. Seems like fictional characters are best. You know very well that no man will ever be as wonderful as Mr. Darcy."

"Captain Wentworth sure knows how to write a letter."

I laughed. "All of Austen's heroes are hot."

"So is Flynn."

"So is Jonathan just in a different way."

Hayley's golden-brown eyes fixed on me. "Mighty convenient that Jonathan showed up in the park at the exact moment someone shot you with that arrow."

"Why do you have to be so suspicious of him?"

"Aren't we suspicious of everyone? Why does he get a pass?"

I tried to throw up my hands and a jolt of pain instantly made me realize my mistake. I took a deep breath and then said, "I guess because he was in New Jersey at the time of the murder. We have proof, that security footage, remember? And why would he want to hurt me? He barely knows me. I'll tell you what though, he continues to help us. He told me he wouldn't say anything to Silas Dale about what happened today."

"Did he? I don't know, Kay. I wonder if he'll come over here tomorrow or stay in Charlottesville and just call you since you're sidelined."

"Sidelined?" I yawned. "I'm not staying in bed all day just because my arm is in a sling, no way."

The hinges of my bedroom door creaked. Hayley and I both jumped.

Cho slid inside, looked at us, and let out a concerned "Meow."

"There's that handsome boy," Hayley said as Cho jumped on the bed. He stretched his neck out to sniff my sling, then withdrew, sneezing.

"Hey sweetheart," I cooed at him. He allowed me to stroke his back. "Are you going to sleep in here tonight and take care of me?"

Cho purred.

"His eyes are amazing," Hayley said. "Every time I see him, I can't get over it. He's like a cat out of a sci-fi film."

"Mmm," I murmured.

Hayley looked at me skeptically. "You're struggling to keep your eyes open. You did pretty well eating with one hand and you're having no problem petting the cat. Why don't I come over first thing in the morning? We can have breakfast and then I'll help you get dressed. While Hugo and Flynn are out looking around the park, we can figure out our next move."

"Sounds like a plan."

"Jane Pawston hasn't had her Tiki Cat Ahi Tuna and Chicken in Chicken Consommé sprinkled with a little grated cheese, and has probably clawed the sofa to punish me."

"I'm sorry, Hayley. I'm exhausted. I guess it was all the carbs."

"The carbs and the fact that you've been shot with an arrow."

"Oh, I almost forgot. At the park when Hugo was helping me put the equipment away, Percy was with him. He said he'd been trying to get in touch with you. He said to tell you that he'd asked after you."

Hayley smiled. "He's a nice guy."

"Don't get too excited now."

"He's too traditional for me, and he knows it. We're going to stay friends. I've noticed him hanging out at Betsy Bell's Happy Fabrics tent an awful lot." Hayley stood up and smoothed the quilt. "You know, Kay, sometimes the future comes from an unexpected direction, and sometimes it comes from right beside you."

I was too tired to figure out what she meant. "Okay, I'll see you in the morning. I doubt you'll be my only visitor. Unless Aunt Adeline gets Brock to do something, Detective Gordon will be on my doorstep bright and early."

As it turned out, I was wrong about that.

Chapter Seventeen

Despite protests from Hayley and Aunt Adeline, after I was dressed in jeans and a soft, cream-colored sweater, I made my way down to the dining room. Since it was Sunday, meals were taken at the formal table. The tall, balsam fir Christmas tree near the fireplace was lit with tiny white lights, perfuming the room and giving it a warm glow.

"Good morning, Miss Kay," Ida Calhoun said putting a small glass of orange juice in front of me. "I've got fresh coffee made, but you need this to swallow your antibiotic."

"You're so thoughtful, Mrs. Calhoun. Thank you," I said and took my pill.

"How about an omelet? You need protein to help your arm heal. I can make one for you too, Miss Hayley."

The big mahogany table already contained a spread of food: grits, biscuits and sausage gravy, bacon, pancakes, toast, and an assortment of butters and jams. Hayley had brought a Regency favorite. Banbury cake was a spiced, oval-shaped, currant-filled pastry. I reached for a piece.

Hayley said, "That's a good idea, Mrs. Calhoun. If you don't mind, Kay and I could share an omelet. I know how big you make them."

"Vegetable and cheese omelet all right?" the older lady asked.

I nodded. "That sounds delicious. Thank you."

While Ida Calhoun returned to the kitchen and cooked, Hayley and I chatted. I'd brought down the old-fashioned, Regency-style newspaper Flynn had given me. "Neil's done a terrific job on this," I said turned the pages with my left hand. "Look at the headline: February 5, 1811 The Regency Act is passed by Parliament, authorizing the Prince of Wales to rule in his father's place as the Prince Regent."

"Our Jane didn't like him much. You know she didn't want to dedicate *Emma* to him, but what could she do when he requested it?" Hayley said, accepting plates from Mrs. Calhoun and putting one in front of me. "When your arm gets better, I'll bring you some arnica gel to put on it. Mama swears by it."

The omelet had been cooked to perfection, and so I told Mrs. Calhoun.

"I'm glad you like it. Did y'all hear they're predicting snow for Tuesday?"

Hayley scoffed. "It's gonna be in the upper fifties later today."

"They're saying a cold front's coming in," I said.

At that moment, Aunt Adeline burst into the room in a flurry of silk. "Who's dead? Kay, thank God you and Hayley are all right.

Where's Hugo? What did I do with my phone? I need to text him and make sure he's alive."

Cho had followed her into the room. He jumped up on the green overstuffed chair beneath the *Irish and Wire Fox Terriers Inspecting a Burrow* painting. Then, as he'd done before, he reached out a paw and tapped the painting while muttering to himself. Aunt Adeline was so upset, she failed to scold him.

"What's happened?" I asked her, feeling a prickle of fear run up my spine. "What are you talking about?"

Hayley and Mrs. Calhoun were staring at Aunt Adeline.

She explained, "I had just finished dressing when I happened to look out the window facing the back field. The white stag was running across the grass toward the woods. I grabbed those binoculars that I keep near my vanity table to make sure it was him and it was!"

Hayley cut her eyes at me.

Mrs. Calhoun said, "Gracious, I'll bring up the hash brown casserole," and headed for the kitchen.

"Come sit, Aunt Adeline. I've got my phone here," I said. "You can—"

But I got no further. The sound of the front door opening and closing, then male voices reached our ears. Hugo, Flynn, and Betsy Bell walked into the room. All three had grim expressions. Betsy Bell's face was tear-stained.

Aunt Adeline gripped the back of her chair. "Thank God you're all okay. I saw the white stag. Who's dead?"

Flynn, looking hotter than a box of firecrackers, had on dark jeans and a teal-colored sweater. He nodded knowingly.

"The white stag never fails to deliver his message. Alexandra Bartholomew was found dead in Dogwood Park."

Everyone spoke at once demanding to know what happened.

Aunt Adeline, composed now that she knew who died, took control. "Please! Y'all sit down, have something to eat. Betsy Bell, you sit by me. You need a hot cup of tea."

"With plenty of sugar," Flynn said. "The best thing for shock."

"Thank you," Betsy Bell whispered. I noticed she wore a pink tracksuit. A white ruffled collar peeked out from under the top.

Percy, looking sharp in khakis and a navy-blue sweater over a pale blue collared shirt emerged from the powder room. "Here now, Betsy Bell. I've dampened this handkerchief with cool water so you can wipe your face." He sat down at the table on her other side.

Betsy Bell raised her eyes to him and accepted the handkerchief. She looked at Percy like little Barrett Leigh had looked at a visiting Santa Claus two weeks earlier at Monday's Country Store.

I was getting whiplash. Alexandra dead. Flynn recommending sugar. Betsy Bell with a crush on Percy. Aunt Adeline's white stag two-for-two. I put my Banbury cake on my plate and reached for my Jane Austen pendant.

Mrs. Calhoun brought the hot hash brown casserole. Hayley took it and scooped out a serving and plated it. She passed it to Hugo who smiled his thanks at her. She continued passing plates around while Flynn, drinking tea with no sugar, spoke.

"Hugo and I went to Dogwood Park to see if we could find any clues as to who shot you with that arrow, Kay. Percy joined us."

"We didn't find anything because Detective Gordon and Officer Fowler were already there checking it out," Hugo said. He took a gulp of coffee, then said, "Percy saw the detective walk toward his car. Gordon had found a bow and was bagging it up as evidence."

"That's right," Percy said. "Flynn suggested we question him, but before we could do so, we heard Betsy Bell scream."

Everyone looked at Betsy Bell. The hot tea and a freshened face had seemed to revive her. "I always go to the park on Sunday mornings before church. I like to feed the ducks. There's a dispenser of food for them near their pond. It's only fifty cents, and you get a big handful." She looked around the table as if seeking approval of this expenditure.

Percy nodded and smiled at her.

I wished she'd get to the point.

"I love to throw the food to them and watch them eat," she continued. Then her expression darkened. Percy put his arm around the back of her chair. "Well, I'd fed them all the food I had and turned to leave when I saw someone lying on one of those iron benches that they have throughout the park. My first thought was that someone didn't have a place to sleep and that they'd slept on the bench. I stepped closer and saw it was a woman with long blonde hair. I wanted to help. We're supposed to help other people. So, I walked toward her but then I saw the blood and realized it was Alexandra and *you know*."

I thought she would start to cry, but then Cho must have rubbed up against her leg as she looked down and said, "What a beautiful cat. May I pet him?"

Aunt Adeline, apparently making an exception to the "No Cho in Public" rule said, "Of course. Excuse me. I'm going to call Brock Winthrop."

Poor Betsy Bell, I thought. First she finds Nathaniel, now Alexandra. Thankfully, Percy kept her distracted with Cho while Flynn continued.

In a low voice, he said, "Alexandra had been stabbed with a stainless-steel knitting needle. I heard one of the county people say it went straight into her heart."

As one, we all turned to look at Betsy Bell. You didn't have to be a knitter to realize that Betsy Bell would sell knitting needles at her store. Fortunately, she was still petting Cho and talking to Percy.

Hayley looked furtively toward the kitchen door, then back at us. "Sharon knits."

"That's right," I said. "She told Flynn and me that she took it up years ago."

Hugo said, "Sharon was at the park too. Said she walks to help control her stress. Owww, Hayley!"

I saw him reach down and rub his leg just as Ida Calhoun came back in the room. "Y'all need anything?"

Our chorus of noes ended with the sound of the back door slamming.

Ida turned and hurried back to the kitchen.

I said, "Bet that's Sharon now. What are we going to do?"

"We don't have enough information yet to know what to do," Flynn said. "Detective Gordon tried to question both Betsy Bell and Sharon, but neither were having it."

"That's good," I said, relieved.

"The medical response team came. They'll have the medical examiner from Harrisonburg examine Alexandra to figure out how and when she was killed. But I heard one of them say the body was still warm," Hugo said.

"That means she hadn't been dead long," Hayley said. "You learn things watching *Vera*."

"Hey, I like *Vera*. Maybe we can watch it together sometime," Hugo said.

Hayley tilted her head at him. "The show's over. They've already aired the last episode."

"There are these things called reruns, Hailstorm," Hugo said.

Before Hayley could flare up, I said, "I didn't like Alexandra, but the image of her laid out on a park bench, dead, is sad. I can hardly believe we've had a second murder in our town."

Flynn sighed. "Yes, it is sad. Then there's the obvious problem of how a second murder will affect the festival."

My face scrunched up on one side. "It'll be all over the web. Maybe people will be so busy with all the events planned they won't pay it any mind."

Flynn gave me a pitying look. "I think we have to consider that we may lose some festival goers."

"I'll keep an eye out for any refund requests on our website," Hayley said.

I groaned.

Aunt Adeline returned to the table. "We're in luck. Brock was already on his way over here from Charlottesville to talk to Kay about the attack on her. He'll be here shortly. Betsy Bell, you stay with us now, you hear? The attorney will want to speak with you about Alexandra."

"Okay, but I don't know what I can tell him. I'd rather super-glue my lips shut than say this but Alexandra wasn't a very nice person," Betsy Bell said.

"I know what you mean, Betsy Bell," I said, "but it's probably best not to say that to the attorney and certainly not to Detective Gordon."

Especially since I'd lay money on the fact that Detective Gordon likely thinks you killed her and Nathaniel Grant. The detective was probably chomping at the bit to arrest you.

Percy asked, "Would y'all mind if I stayed here while Betsy Bell is questioned? I know it wouldn't be appropriate for me to be in the room, but if I could wait out on the terrace or something . . ."

"That's very kind, Percy," Betsy Bell said. "Would it be all right, Mrs. Starling?"

Aunt Adeline looked slowly from Percy to Betsy Bell. "Yes, I think that would work out just fine."

Hayley checked the time on her phone. "It's almost ten o'clock. My sales tent opens at eleven. I've got to go over to the bakery and make sure Valeria has everything ready. Then we've got to lug all those food tubs over. I'm sure Sharon won't be able to help."

"I'll help," Hugo said.

"You'll eat half my stock," Hayley countered.

"I'll leave you a few cookies to sell," Hugo said with a grin.

"Okay, fine. Beggars can't be choosers," Hayley grumbled. "Kay, you need to take it easy today. Don't forget to ice your arm."

I agreed and she and Hugo left, bickering the whole way out the door.

Percy helped Aunt Adeline clear the table. I wondered what was going on in the kitchen between Sharon and her mother.

Chapter Eighteen

F ifteen minutes later, Brock Winthrop arrived in another expensive suit and a red bow-tie dotted with green Christmas trees. Aunt Adeline let him in and took Cho back upstairs. I greeted the attorney and introduced him to Percy. They talked briefly about Percy's horse farm and his intention of working with Hugo before Aunt Adeline returned and showed Percy out to the sunroom.

When they were gone, we heard a loud cry of "Yes!" come from the kitchen.

"Flynn, would you come with me to the kitchen?" I asked. "I need an ice pack. My arm hurts."

"Yes."

Brock said, "I'll want to talk to you about that injury, Kay."

"I'll be around," I told him. "Excuse us, please."

We left Brock, Aunt Adeline, and Betsy Bell to talk about the latest murder and went into the kitchen. Ida was busy putting together a pot of soup.

But it was the smile on Sharon's face that stole the air from my lungs leaving me momentarily breathless. Sharon never smiled.

At least, I'd never seen her smile. I'd once asked Hayley if she'd seen Sharon smile and she hadn't either. Now, Sharon's eyes were narrowed and glinted with cold satisfaction while her lips spread in a closed mouth smirk.

When she saw us, her expression instantly became reserved. "Hello Flynn, Kay. I heard about the attack on you, Kay. How's your arm this morning?"

"Hurting, I'm afraid. I came down for an ice pack," I said and turned to the fridge to hunt around in the freezer.

Flynn leaned over me and retrieved an ice bag full of cubes. I caught a whiff of a woodsy, amber scent before he closed the freezer door and stepped back. He tucked the ice bag inside my sling then he looked at Sharon. "You had a shock this morning, Sharon. Are you all right?"

Ida tapped the spoon on the lid of the soup pot, placed the spoon on the stove, and then stood next to her daughter, facing us.

"I'm okay," Sharon said with a shrug. "I mean it wasn't what I was expecting to see when I went for a morning run, but I didn't know Alexandra."

"I've been a slacker when it comes to my morning run," I said casually. "Do you normally run in Dogwood Park?"

"I don't run on a regular basis. Only when I'm super-stressed," Sharon said. "See, I had to tell Palmer about Nate being dead. I'd put it off until the weekend so I wouldn't disrupt his classes."

Ida put a comforting hand on her daughter's arm.

"It couldn't have been pleasant for you or your son," Flynn said sympathetically.

"No. Like I told y'all, they didn't have a relationship, but you still grieve what might have been. It's weird, but there it is. Anyway, I called Palmer last night and told him. He took it okay."

"But you still felt bad about it this morning," I said.

Sharon nodded. "I did, because Palmer has huge student loans. I guess I'd somehow hoped Nate would help him eventually. Not very logical of me, I know."

She and her mother exchanged a look.

Then Sharon said, "Life is funny though. I just got a call from an attorney I hired saying that Palmer is the sole beneficiary of Nate's $500,000 life insurance policy."

"Wow," I said. "That's terrific news for Palmer!"

"It certainly is," Ida Calhoun said. "Nate must have forgotten to change the beneficiary on the policy. He was a nasty man and probably would have left the money to his latest bimbo."

"Ironic, isn't it? After all these years of Nate flat out refusing to help financially with Palmer's needs, he dies and Palmer is taken care of!" Sharon said and then started laughing. "Oh, how he'd hate that!" She laughed again.

Ida remained stoic.

"I don't suppose you saw anyone at the park who might want to harm Alexandra," Flynn said.

Sharon shook her head. "Like I said, I didn't know Alexandra. I mean, I saw Betsy Bell. I've heard about their argument over the dresses and maybe Nate. Betsy Bell doesn't seem capable of murder. Then again, she's the one who's found two bodies. They say the person that finds a dead body is likely the murderer. Who knows?"

"Not me," I said briskly. "Flynn, I usually put out food and water for the birds, chipmunks, and squirrels. Would you help me since I'm down an arm?"

"Yes."

We left Ida and Sharon in the kitchen and went outside and crossed the flagstone terrace. The sun was out, warming the winter air.

At the brick folly, Flynn looked over the bags of mixed bird seed, sunflower seeds, unsalted peanuts, and gallons of water. "You're a country girl at heart, aren't you?"

"I don't know. I never thought about it. I just love seeing the birds, squirrels, and chipmunks. Although I do have one pesky crow," I said.

I directed him as to which bowls and feeders held what. He pushed up the sleeves of his sweater and got to work. Above, birds and squirrels started gathering on the branches of the maple trees.

"A pesky crow?"

"Yes, his name is Henry Tilney after a character in Jane Austen's *Northanger Abbey*. He sometimes leaves me little presents, but more recently he's been dive-bombing my hats. I can't complain too much as the last time was yesterday at Dogwood Park. Tilney swooped down toward me and that's when I lost my footing and fell just as whoever shot me with an arrow."

Flynn put an empty gallon of water in the recycling bin. "A crow saved you from a more serious injury, then?"

"Maybe." I smiled. Then I felt the smile fade from my face.

"Kay, what is it?"

"Yesterday, I heard Tilney caw then I heard something else, but I can't remember what it was. Or maybe, I was supposed to have heard something, but didn't. I can't remember!" I exclaimed, frustrated.

He came to my side. "Be gentle with yourself. It's not been twenty-four hours since you were attacked."

"And less than that since Alexandra was murdered. Flynn, I'm scared that Detective Gordon is going to arrest Betsy Bell."

"That would be foolish. No one believes Betsy Bell could kill anyone. I don't like saying this, but I think Sharon is not what she seemed during our interview at the Golden Age Diner."

"That thought went through my mind when I saw her smile."

"And the laughter. Quite chilling, wasn't it? What if Nathaniel had taken out an insurance policy whilst he and Alexandra were talking about going into business together? It's common practice for business partners to have life insurance policies on one another. He makes Palmer the next in line to receive the funds if Alexandra dies. It gives Sharon a motive for murder."

I flinched at the idea. "Yes, it does. She loves Palmer dearly. She wouldn't want him to have student loans weighing him down in debt for years on end. But how would she know about the life insurance policy in the first place?"

"Perhaps she didn't see Nathaniel dead on the floor and run back down the steps to the Assembly Rooms as she told us. Instead, she finally confronts her ex after all these years. It's a blazing row. He tells her he's considering leaving Virginia, going into business with Alexandra, even has a life insurance policy for her. She grabs Betsy Bell's scissors and kills him in the heat of the moment and out of a strong desire to help Palmer."

"Then all she has to do is eliminate Alexandra," I said in a faint voice.

"Precisely. Even if she didn't have an argument with Nathaniel during which he told her about the policy, she may have learnt about it through Alexandra herself."

"Through Alexandra?"

"Sharon might have approached her about Nathaniel on the pretext of warning her of his true character. Alexandra brags that he loves her and they're going into business together. She mentions the life insurance policy to drive the point home. I don't know if she did or not. I'm only speculating. Sharon also mentioned that she had an attorney."

He ran a hand through his hair. A few bird seeds stuck in the dark strands. I had to resist a strong urge to reach up and brush them away.

"Flynn, remember Aunt Adeline told us that Ida Calhoun tried to say that she'd been to see Nathaniel the day he was killed."

He snapped his fingers. "Yes. I believe Mrs. Calhoun thought her daughter may have murdered her ex. She tried to shield her. Sorry to say, it's looking bleak for Sharon, in my opinion."

I said, "I thought Alexandra was our killer. Now that she's dead, I'm worried that Sharon committed both murders. How can I feel this way? I'm sorry for Sharon, she's one of our townspeople, and I don't want to think she's a killer. Yet everything is pointing to her now. I want to see justice done."

"You're a caring person, Kay. That's why you're conflicted." He pulled out his phone and checked the time. "Right. I have to go. I've agreed to judge the Romantic Letter Writing competition. Francie is holding it at the Golden Age Diner. They're closing to the public for two hours."

Who decided Flynn would be a good judge of what's romantic?

"I'm sorry to miss that, but I can't write well with my left hand. Besides, I have to speak with Brock." I paused, then said, "Will you come to dinner tonight? You know Aunt Adeline always holds a big dinner on Sunday nights."

"That's a family occasion, surely."

"Well, I'm inviting you. Aunt Adeline is making her famous crab cakes. I'm sure Guthrie will be there and Hayley if she can make it."

"Thank you. I accept your invitation. Do you need anything before I leave?"

"No, I'm going back inside," I told him. My gaze strayed to the bird seed in his hair. "Sunday dinners are at four o'clock."

Don't touch his hair, Kay!

"All right." He glanced back at the folly. "I think your friends will be having their own Sunday feast."

I watched him carefully. "Hugo thinks I'm silly, because I talk to them."

Flynn's brows drew together. "I wonder why he thinks that. When I was in England, I had a hedgehog that always came to me when I was in the garden. Sometimes I brought him worms. I'd talk to him about the weather. Missed the little bugger when I came to the States."

I grinned. Then I reached up and brushed the seeds from his hair.

Inside the house, only Ida remained in the kitchen.

"You need anything, Miss Kay?" she asked me.

"No, I'm just going to empty my ice bag in the sink," I told her.

After doing so, I walked out of the kitchen and went upstairs, wondering if I should tell Brock about Sharon and deciding against it for now.

My phone rang. It was Jonathan. I paused at the top of the stairs.

"Kay, how are you? You don't have to answer. I'd like to come over to find out if you don't mind."

I could almost see his sheepish smile. "Hi, Jonathan. When will you be here?"

"Say around two-thirty or so. I've got work to do or I'd come right now. Should we meet somewhere or is it safe for me to come to the house?" he asked with a nervous chuckle.

"Come to the house. See you soon." I ended the call.

In the dining room, Aunt Adeline and Brock sat at the table.

"Betsy Bell gone home?" I asked, smiling thanks at Brock as he pulled out a chair for me.

"She left with Percy a few minutes ago," Aunt Adeline said.

Brock questioned me about what happened at Dogwood Park the day before. He wanted a list of people who'd taken archery lessons from me. He asked me about the time between when I went to leave the park and when I returned to Starling Farm.

"This Jonathan Warren who helped you. He's from Dale Casino Resorts?" he asked.

"Yes," I said. "He seems honest and he's been supportive of me. He made no bones about telling me that he had been sent back down here to give a report to Silas Dale on the status of the festival after the murder." I left out the part about how he'd broken the rules to find out who Nathaniel Grant's ex-wife was.

"Jonathan has a crush on Kay. He's been sweet on her since the first time he came down here from New Jersey," Aunt Adeline said. "I don't like who he works for, but I can't dismiss how caring he was toward Kay when he found her at the park and subsequently took her to the hospital."

Brock wrote notes. "You have no idea who—"

The sound of the doorbell interrupted him.

Aunt Adeline rose. "Are you expecting anyone, Kay?"

"Not until later. Jonathan said he would stop by to see how I am."

Brock continued writing notes while we waited for Aunt Adeline to come back.

I felt a jolt of surprise when she entered the room with a suited Detective Gordon.

Aunt Adeline introduced him to Brock, then asked him to sit down. "Can I bring you something to drink? Coffee? A soda?"

"No thank you, Mrs. Starling, and I prefer to stand," he said. His Voice of Authority was dialed up to ten. "I'd like Miss Starling to take me through the incident at Dogwood Park yesterday where she was injured."

I made swift work of it, glancing now and then over at Brock who was listening intently.

"And you don't know who might want to hurt you?" the detective asked me.

"No."

"Someone you might have been questioning in your amateur investigation of Nathaniel Grant's murder?" He said the words "amateur investigation" with more than a hint of derision.

"No," I answered a bit more stiffly.

"You admit that you continue to act as if you are a member of my department interrogating suspects."

"What's bothering you more: the fact that I'm speaking to our neighbors about the crime, or the fact that I'm not sharing what I find out with you?" I asked.

"It's your duty to inform my department of any information that might lead us to the murderer," Detective Gordon said indignantly.

"Maybe I would if you weren't so hostile to me and my friends! If you hadn't already decided that Betsy Bell Ward is a cold-blooded killer!"

He pointed a finger at me. "You might think you're a plucky heroine from one of your favorite author's books, but I'll have you up on a charge obstruction of justice if I find out you have useful information and are withholding it."

Aunt Adeline shot him a look so sharp it could have broken up the iceberg that sunk the Titanic.

Brock Winthrop rose. "Detective Gordon, you are harassing my client while she is recovering from an attempt on her life. This meeting is over."

Derek Gordon made to leave, then turned back around and spoke directly to me, "I'm confident that I'll be making an arrest in the murders of Nathaniel Grant *and* Alexandra Bartholomew within the next twenty-four hours. Turns out, I never needed your help."

Chapter Nineteen

After the detective left, I laid on my bed with a cup of tea and Cho for company. I felt chilled, whether it was from Detective Gordon's words or the fresh ice bag in my sling, it was hard to tell. I pulled my Jane Austen book covers quilt closer around me. "What do you think, Cho? Have I somehow misread the situation? Could sweet Betsy Bell have a dark side?"

Cho kneaded his paws on a *Northanger Abbey* square before turning around three times and laying down with his head propped up on my calf.

"My thinking is too gothic? You're right," I said with a sigh.

A knock sounded at my door. "Come in!"

Ida Calhoun opened the door and peeked around the wood frame. "I brought you some soup. You feel like you can eat?"

"Sure," I answered, struggling to sit up in bed. Then I saw she had a tray. "I'm feeling useless here with one working arm."

"Don't worry about that," she said.

Before I knew it, she had me settled comfortably with a bed tray containing a bowl of ham and potato soup, slices of warm French bread, and a fruit salad of clementines, kiwi, pears, apples, and pomegranate.

Cho lifted his nose and sniffed.

I smiled. "Wow, this looks delicious. Look how pretty that fruit salad is."

Mrs. Calhoun nodded. "That's a new recipe I'm trying out to fix for Christmas Eve. It has a honey lime poppy seed dressing. Now, are you up to date on your antibiotic? Let me take that ice bag for you."

As Mrs. Calhoun fussed over me, I couldn't help but feel ashamed that I thought her daughter had killed two people. What would happen to this kind, older lady who'd been so close to my family if her daughter were arrested for murder? What about Sharon's son, Palmer? First his father abandons the family, then his mother goes to prison? My appetite fled.

"Is anything wrong, Miss Kay? You're not eating."

"My mind wandered." I picked up my spoon and tasted my soup. "Mmm, this is wonderful. You know I love your ham and potato soup."

She smiled and closed the door behind her. I dutifully ate all the food she'd prepared for me and must have dozed off afterward. The next thing I knew, Aunt Adeline was taking the tray from my lap. There was no sign of Cho.

"I didn't want to wake you, but Jonathan Warren is downstairs waiting for you in the sunroom," she said.

"I think that antibiotic is wearing me out. I'll freshen up and be right down."

"Find out where he was last night," Aunt Adeline said. "Covering our bases, Kay. Remember that everyone is a suspect."

At the entrance to the sunroom, I took in the sight of Jonathan, wearing a red plaid shirt and jeans and looking out across the grass. I had to admit that it was a nice view.

The sunroom had diamond paned windows and matching sliding French doors. A sofa and two comfy chairs were made of bamboo with thick Kelly-green cushions and printed throw cushions. An abundance of ferns and spider plants combined with a square, bright yellow dining table and chairs made for a relaxed atmosphere. A tall, standing, decorative bamboo birdcage—birdless—stood in one corner. I chuckled when I saw Cho stretched out across the birdcage roof.

The sound brought Jonathan's attention to me. He turned with a big grin that allowed me to admire his boyish dimples. "Kay, how are you?" he asked coming toward me.

"I'm fine. Everyone is spoiling me."

"That's as it should be," he said, moving to the sofa. "I brought you a poinsettia and a little something else. Forgive me, I didn't have time to wrap it, so it's still in the bag."

My eyes went from the poinsettia plant to Cho whose tail was twitching. Poinsettia plants, toxic to cats and dogs, were never a part of Starling Farm's Christmas decorations. I couldn't be rude, but would have to make sure Cho didn't try for a nibble. I'd give the plant to Ida Calhoun to take home after Jonathan left.

I accepted the bag Jonathan held out and opened it. "This is funny!" I shook out the sweatshirt that depicted the outline of a person wearing a sling and the words, "I Do My Own Stunts" on it. "You didn't have to bring me anything, but thank you."

Ida Calhoun stepped into the room, lips pursed in disapproval. She set out a tray with glass mugs of hot apple cider with cinnamon sticks and a plate of salted caramel cookies.

"That looks and smells delicious, Mrs. Calhoun," I said. "Have you met Jonathan Warren?"

"I know who he is," she said and looked away. Unfortunately, her gaze landed on the poinsettia plant then swung to Cho.

Another warm welcome for Jonathan at Starling Farm!

Jonathan shifted his weight and looked at the floor.

I had to avert disaster. "Mrs. Calhoun, would you please take that lovely poinsettia plant to the kitchen and give it some water? Jonathan brought it for me and I want to keep it healthy."

"I believe they watered it at the florist, Kay," Jonathan said meekly.

Mrs. Calhoun bent and swept the plant into her arms. "I'll certainly take it away."

Jonathan and I sat next to one another on the sofa and drank our cider and ate cookies. Tension hung like a cloud over the room. I avoided talking about the reception he received whenever he visited. And I avoided talking about Alexandra. Instead, our conversation centered on Christmas plans (he would be with his sister), whether or not snow was coming (I doubted it), and extravagant Christmas light displays we'd seen.

Cho jumped down from the birdcage and slinked toward us, his belly low, his amazing eyes on Jonathan. He let out a low hiss.

Even the cat!

I patted the cushion next to me. Luckily, Cho gracefully leapt up beside me and laid down.

"I suppose you've heard," I finally said.

He nodded regretfully. "The news about Miz Bartholomew is online."

"Dominating the local news, no doubt. I haven't looked."

"Don't. Someone posted a photo of Ms. Bartholomew deceased on a park bench. It's graphic, and it's gone viral."

"What?" I exclaimed. "How could someone have a photo like that?"

"I'm as sure as sure can be that it's fake. It's a manipulated image, Photoshopped or AI. Easy to do nowadays and people can be ghouls."

"Have you spoken with Silas Dale about this latest murder?"

"No. On Sundays, he plays golf with his cronies and doesn't tolerate anyone interrupting his game. I reckon I'll hear from him soon. It's after three-thirty. He'll be wanting something to eat and a cocktail while I brief him."

I remembered Aunt Adeline's suggestion that I find out where Jonathan was last night. "What did you do last night after you left here? Anything fun going on in Charlottesville?"

The words were hardly out of my mouth when I saw the sadness in his eyes. He knew I didn't completely trust him. I felt heat rise to my face and looked away.

"I had Chinese take-out and watched a movie. *The Martian.* You know I like outer space. I like you too, Kay, and wish you had faith in me."

I turned back to him only to find his face close to mine. He was going to kiss me. He was moving slowly as if asking for permission. My heart rate kicked up. I wasn't sure I wanted him to kiss me. I moved my head away.

Suddenly, Cho stood and let out a loud yowl. Bowie raced into the room, barking at Cho and jumping left, then right. Hugo rushed in and grabbed the dog's collar. Aunt Adeline followed and grasped Cho and took him away.

It was then that I saw Flynn standing framed in the doorway to the sunroom, a look of distaste marring his handsome features. Without a word, he turned and walked away.

"I can see that I'd better leave," Jonathan said, standing.

I rose. "Jonathan—"

"No, don't say anything. Maybe I'll have better luck once whoever is responsible for these killings is caught. I'll text you, if that's agreeable, to see how you're doing. I worry about you, Kay."

"You're coming to the ball on Tuesday night, aren't you? It's our big celebration of Jane's 250th birthday."

"It sounds like y'all will do Miz Austen proud. It'd be best if I stayed away, though."

"Oh, please come and dance with me. I might make a comical partner with my arm in a sling, but we can try."

He grinned. "Sounds like a perfect dance, but I'll take a raincheck."

Dinner was a subdued affair. Ida Calhoun had gone home with Sharon. Aunt Adeline had free reign to make her crab cakes. Josie helped her put everything on the table. I felt useless with my arm out of commission.

Hayley had promised to have dinner with Serenity. Since her mama was normally a loner, keeping to her painting and her books, Hayley wouldn't dream of backing out of the invitation.

Hugo had eaten steadily and said little. When asked, he said, "Percy took Betsy Bell to a bistro in Harrisonburg for dinner. Hope it goes okay."

I thought for a moment, then said, "I bet it will. Let me know if you hear anything. Aunt Adeline, these crab cakes are insanely good."

"Thank you, Kay," she said and went back to talking with Guthrie about plans for Christmas Day.

Flynn had complimented the cook and then had concentrated on his food.

I knew he disapproved of my friendship with Jonathan. Was it even a friendship? We were acquaintances at best, I thought.

Sure Kay, another sixty seconds and you would have tasted caramel and it wouldn't have been on the cookies.

I blushed at my thoughts earning me an inquiring gaze from Flynn.

"I was thinking about the Romantic Letters class at the Golden Age diner. How did it go?" I asked him.

"I'm certain that if I wished to compose a letter of affection to a lady in the Regency era, I'd have all the skills I'd need," he answered me tersely. Then he turned to Hugo. "Fancy a beer at Gator's after we help with the washing up?"

Aunt Adeline didn't demur at his offer to do the dishes. She and Guthrie went to sit by the Christmas tree with mugs of hot chocolate. She'd asked me to join them, but I pled fatigue and went to my room. I wasn't fibbing.

As much as I wanted to sleep, I lay in bed with my mind playing over the conversations I'd had with Alexandra and Sharon, the glee Sharon expressed when she found out about Nate's life insurance policy, Betsy Bell's sweet words about wanting to help what she'd thought was a homeless person, Detective Gordon's horrid attitude and words to me, my almost kiss with Jonathan. Over all of it was an urgent need to know who had committed two murders.

Round and round my thoughts went until I finally drifted off remembering how silky Flynn's hair had felt when I'd brushed away the bird seed.

Chapter Twenty

M onday morning at ten o'clock, I was clad in a sprigged muslin Regency gown, spencer jacket, and bonnet sans feather. I approached the red double doors of the church hall. The building was white clapboard and long, big enough to hold both the Regency Breakfast and the Silent Auction I wanted to check out.

It was a gray day and chilly so I was happy to enter the warm room, adorned with the standard fresh greenery and tiny white lights. From somewhere, a symphony by Ignaz Pleyel, one of Austen's favorite composers, played.

On one side of the hall, festively decorated long tables had been set up where festival attendees in costume and in regular clothing were enjoying the delights of a Public Breakfast just as Jane would have enjoyed in say, Bath. Bread rolls, toasted fruit cake, teas, coffee, and cakes were offered by servers in Regency dress.

On the other side of the room, tables against the walls displayed items up for auction. Everything Austen related from silk shawls to reproductions of the crosses both Jane and her sister, Cassandra, wore, to an early edition copy of *Persuasion*. My heart rate kicked up when I saw it as it reminded me of Aunt Adeline's treasured copy of *Sense and Sensibility*.

At the end of one of the long tables was a painting of Jane Austen. The artist was Serenity, and it had gathered many admirers. Serenity herself sat at a small table. She'd been creating a silhouette for a gentleman who was paying her for her efforts. As soon as the gentleman walked away, Hayley, also dressed in sprigged muslin, put a take-out cup and a plate with a pastry in front of her mother. Aunt Adeline walked over and started chatting with them.

"Hey, Kay, how's the arm?"

I turned to see my brother Neil, camera around his neck, holding a stack of the old-fashioned newspapers he'd printed out mimicking a Regency newspaper of 1811. Darkness under his eyes indicated he'd not slept well.

"Better this morning. How about you?"

He let out a sigh. "Have you looked at the online news this morning?"

"No, I denied myself that pleasure in favor of sleeping in."

"I wrestled with my journalist's conscience, but in the end, I wrote an op-ed about the murders stating that they were the result of personal conflicts, not a danger to the public at large, and not, as others have suggested, the work of a serial killer."

My jaw dropped. "A serial killer? Who said that?"

"The slimier British tabloids have picked up on the story and fantasized it," he said grimly. "Trouble is, I've seen some of the bigger USA media sensationalizing the story, too. I should have stuck to stating the facts only, but I couldn't let other journalists jump on the fear-mongering bandwagon."

"Thanks, Neil," I said. "I'm surprised none of those other so-called journalists haven't shown up here."

"Probably couldn't find us." Neil looked around, then said, "We've got a full crowd in here and there were plenty of people at the sales tents when I walked over."

"Yes, I was thankful to see that too."

He leaned closer. "Look, Kay, I can't tell you how I know this, but there's a report that Silas Dale is either in town or on his way."

My eyes widened. "He's premature in his expectations. I hope Jonathan Warren hasn't led him to believe he'll get his way with his awful casino resort plans."

Neil shook his head. "Not Jonathan. Coralie Bouchard. You didn't hear that, understand? You know nothing about it."

I nodded. "I hope Mayor Buckalew hasn't been swayed by Coralie."

"That, I don't know. See you later. I've got papers to distribute and photos to take. We want some cheerful evidence of people having a big time at the festival to put online and hopefully get picked up by news outlets."

I stood in the middle of the room with my fingers grasping my Jane Austen pendant. This was it. Jane Austen Town had failed. Coralie had convinced the mayor that all our efforts had been in vain. Were they going to accept Silas Dale's offer and then spring it on the townspeople? Jonathan had said the casino resort wouldn't happen if the people didn't want it, but was he wrong? Where was Flynn? I needed to text him.

A male voice close by startled me out of my doomsday musings.

"What do you want for Christmas, young lady? Seems you were thinking mighty hard about it."

I turned to see Father Christmas. I struggled to determine who he actually was beyond the gray beard and somewhat tattered red cap, but I didn't recognize him. He waited patiently now for my answer, a kind look in his brown eyes.

All my worries bubbled to the surface. "I want Jane Austen Town to be successful and for all my neighbors and friends to be happy. I don't want anyone to struggle to keep a roof over their head or to put food on the table or fear the bill when they go to the doctor. I want us all to work together as a community. And," I paused fearing I would not be able to say the next words. "I want the person who has taken two lives to be caught and punished."

He listened intently, then gave me a gentle smile and nodded.

"Kay! Oh, I'm so glad I found you."

I swung around. Betsy Bell, flushed with happiness, stepped up to me with a small pink gift bag in her hands. "Good morning, Betsy Bell," I managed. "I hear you had a lovely dinner last night. Have you met Father Christmas?" I went to introduce her, but Father Christmas was gone. I raised my chin looking over people's heads to see if I could find him with no luck.

Betsy Bell hadn't seemed to notice. She giggled. "Percy took me to Le Professeur Bistro all the way over in Harrisonburg. I've never been to a bistro before. I had the best roast chicken. Oh, but I hear you have a fella courting you, Kay. Jonathan Warren?"

"We're just friends," I said.

"You'd make a cute couple," Betsy Bell said. "He wandered into my shop the other day. Didn't buy anything, but that's okay. He has perfect manners."

"He does."

"Well, I have to get back to my sales tent. You won't believe it, but Percy asked me to the Jane Austen Birthday Ball tomorrow night, and I don't have a dress," she said and giggled. "I've sold them all, so I'm spending every free moment sewing one for to-morrow night."

"That's wonderful news, Betsy Bell. Where's Percy today?"

"He had to go back to his horse farm, but he'll be in Jane Austen Town tomorrow afternoon. Oh, silly me. I almost forgot why I came to find you." She reached into the pink gift bag she held and pulled out a gorgeous length of off-white lace that had been sewed into a triangular shape. "See," she said, holding it up. "I made it for you. It's to go over your sling for the ball tomorrow night. Not that there's anything wrong with the sling you have on now. It's just that I know you'll look pretty in your sea-green silk dress, and this lace sling will complement it."

I gave her a quick hug with my good arm. "You are the sweetest, most thoughtful friend. Thank you so much."

"You like it?"

"I love it and will be thrilled to wear it."

"Okay, great! Let's put it back in the bag so it won't get soiled."

She had just closed the gift bag and handed it to me when there was a commotion from the doors to the hall.

Detective Gordon, Officer Fowler, and two uniformed deputies filed into the room and headed right for us. A sudden silence came over the room. People stopped what they were doing to stare.

All at once, the officers reached us. Detective Gordon said, "Betsy Bell Ward, I am placing you under arrest for the murders of Nathaniel Grant and Alexandra Bartholomew."

No! Oh, no!

"But I didn't kill them, Derek," Betsy Bell said, more confused than anything else. "Someone used my good scissors to kill him, but it wasn't me."

He went on without responding. "You have the right to remain silent. Anything you say can and will be used against you in a court of law. You have the right to an attorney."

Flynn appeared out of nowhere. "Do not speak to them without Brock Winthrop, Betsy Bell. Say nothing."

Now there was fear in Betsy Bell's eyes.

Aunt Adeline and Hayley rushed over. Hayley gave Detective Gordon a look of loathing. Aunt Adeline, lines of worry creasing her forehead, repeated Flynn's words. "Don't talk to anyone without Brock, Betsy Bell. It'll be all right."

I found my voice. "Don't do this," I said to Detective Gordon. "You're arresting the wrong woman. I have information you need."

He ignored me.

Officer Fowler moved. She pulled Betsy Bell's hands around her back and snapped handcuffs around her wrists.

Betsy Bell let out a moan and fainted. Flynn caught her head before it hit the floor.

"Look what you've done, Derek!" Hayley yelled.

"Don't think for one second that I won't arrest you too, Hayley Conner. Stay out of my way," Derek Gordon commanded.

"Don't you *dare* speak to my daughter that way, Derek," Serenity said.

"All of you need to step back," he commanded.

None of us moved.

Officer Fowler spoke into her walkie talkie. "We need medical assistance at the church hall, stat."

Flynn had been talking in a low voice to Betsy Bell as she regained consciousness. Gently, he steadied her and helped her to stand. She was off-balance since she was handcuffed.

"She needs a glass of water," Aunt Adeline said.

Officer Fowler took over. "I have her now."

With Officer Fowler on one side and a deputy on the other, they led a dazed Betsy Bell away.

Everyone in the hall resumed talking and eating.

Serenity said, "Don't look at me in that tone of voice, Hayley." She proceeded to give Hayley a talking to for her outburst.

Aunt Adeline spoke rapidly into her phone.

I said to Flynn, "Come with me. We need to talk."

He took the few steps away with me so we couldn't be overheard. He looked down at me over his aquiline nose and said, "Yes?"

"Wait, are you angry at me?"

"What do you want to speak with me about?"

"What just happened, duh," I said, allowing my own anger to show. "We have to help Betsy Bell. We have to tell Detective Gordon what we know about Sharon. He has to know all the facts. This isn't about how we feel about Sharon or Ida Calhoun anymore. We have to tell him."

"I think we should tell Brock Winthrop first."

"Why? They will put Betsy Bell in a jail cell. She won't be able to handle that. We have to go to the police station *now*."

"You think Gordon will listen to us and then magically release Betsy Bell on our word alone? He must have some sort of evidence against Betsy Bell, or he wouldn't have arrested her."

"But what evidence?"

"We don't know. Brock will find out. They will have to tell him, I expect, since he's her attorney of record. My point is, we mustn't act in haste. What if Gordon listens to us and then arrests us for withholding evidence? We wouldn't be much help to Betsy Bell then."

"I just don't want Betsy Bell locked up!"

"Neither do I. Let's speak to Adeline and see how we can lay everything before Brock and allow him decide how to proceed."

"Did I hear my name?" Aunt Adeline said, coming to stand with us.

"Is Brock Winthrop going to get Betsy Bell released?" I asked.

"He's on his way over." She shook her head. "Even though Derek said he would arrest someone, I still couldn't believe it when he came for Betsy Bell like that. Right in the middle of this Regency Breakfast. Seems like he wanted to make a show of it."

I exchanged a look with Flynn.

"Aunt Adeline," I began. "We need to speak with you on a sensitive subject. There's a table for four over there. Let's sit down."

Between us, Flynn and I explained everything we'd learned about Sharon and shared our suspicions.

She frowned. "Lord, what a mess. As close as Ida and I are, I don't know Sharon very well. She's mighty reserved. I do know she loves Palmer to death. They both do."

"I need to go to the police station and tell Derek what I know so he'll release Betsy Bell," I insisted.

"I think it's a decision for Brock Winthrop to make," Flynn said. "He knows the laws. He'll know what's best."

"Kay, I think Flynn's right. Brock will be here soon. He's calling me after he's finished at the police station. I'll tell him we need to speak with him urgently."

Her phone rang.

"Excuse me. It's Buster Buckalew. Let me see what he wants."

She answered the call. I could tell the mayor was giving her an earful as she didn't speak, but her eyebrows rose and her mouth tightened. Finally, she said, "You were right to call me—calm down, Buster. Take a deep breath and don't sign anything. I'll be there in five minutes."

She ended the call and said, "More trouble. Silas Dale is in town staying at Coralie Bouchard's house. Jonathan Warren is there, too. Buster says they're pressuring him to sign off on the casino resort. Let's go."

Chapter
Twenty-One

C oralie Bouchard's house sat on a double lot on a side street. The Colonial Revival house had a widow's walk, probably one of the reasons Coralie decided to buy it being a widow herself. It was white brick with black shutters. I spared a second to admire the pristine landscaping and the multitude of flowers, most of them in various shades of coral, that surrounded the three-story house.

The three of us had walked from the church hall. Aunt Adeline rang the bell. A uniformed maid answered. Aunt Adeline, nice as pie, fibbed and said we were expected. We walked in and the maid motioned us to follow her.

As we passed the grand spiral staircase, I noticed that chairs, footstools, sofas, loveseats were all done in shades of Coralie's signature coral with some green accents among the Federal style antiques. Tasteful greenery added a festive spirit.

However, when the maid opened the double doors to the dining room, I saw the space had exploded with Christmas decorations.

Besides the tall Christmas tree with flashing multi-color lights and masses of wrapped boxes underneath, the top of the sideboard had been cleared and transformed into a crammed mass of mythical Christmas village buildings placed without rhyme or reason and sitting on thick, fake snow. Wide red, velvet ribbons with oversized silver balls had been draped from the ceiling, crisscrossing the room. Dolls from around the world wearing traditional Christmas attire clustered in extra dining room chairs set along the wall with four-foot-tall wooden Nutcrackers guarding them. The fireplace mantel had ceramic Christmas trees in white and green lined up between two big, tall red candles. On either side of the fireplace stood a blow mold Santa Claus and a blow mold snowman—both lit.

Mayor Buckalew, Coralie Bouchard, Silas Dale, and Jonathan Warren sat around the dining room table, the center of which sported Rudolph the Red-Nosed Reindeer pulling a sleigh filled with bright green and bright red pretzels.

"What are you three doing here?" Silas Dale asked rudely. He had on slacks and sports jacket as opposed to Jonathan who wore a suit and tie. Two sets of papers sat on the table in front of the casino resort owner.

"Just look at poor Kay," Mayor Buckalew said. "I told y'all to cancel those archery lessons."

"*I* am the one who told *you* that," Coralie corrected.

"I'm okay, thank you, Mayor," I said.

Without being asked to, Aunt Adeline pulled out a chair and sat down. Flynn and I did the same. She said, "I'll get right to the point, Mr. Dale. Jane Austen Town has had its troubles, it's true, but we are not giving up."

In sharp contrast to the Christmas cheer around her, Coralie had on a black dress. "Silas, I don't know why my maid allowed these people in. I'll speak with her."

My fingers found my Jane Austen pendant. "Coralie, if I may call you that since we're all neighbors," I began. "I understand you've brought Mr. Dale down to Virginia on a fool's errand, haven't you? No one has said we'll be taking up his offer to turn our town into a casino resort."

My eyes went from Coralie's furious gaze to Jonathan's guarded smile. It was difficult to look at Silas Dale's snake eyes.

Jonathan said, "Kay, Mr. Dale and I were led to believe that the tide had turned now that there's been two murders during the festival."

Before I could answer him, Flynn said, "You're quite mistaken, Mr. Warren. This is a tightknit community with shared values. No one has even mentioned taking up your offer."

Mayor Buckalew wiped his brow with a monogrammed handkerchief. "He's right about the town. Neighbors helping neighbors, that's what I always say."

Silas Dale's black eyes bore into the mayor's. "No man makes a fool out of me."

"Certainly not," Coralie said crisply. "It's clear to everyone with two eyes in their head that this Jane Austen experiment has failed.

Mayor, on behalf of the town, we need to sign off on Mr. Dale's generous offer." She pulled a set of papers from in front of Silas Dale toward her, picked up a pen, and signed her name with a flourish.

Had I failed Aunt Adeline after all? I found myself staring into the eyes of a Dutch doll complete with wooden shoes carrying Christmas tulips.

"Walter Buckalew, the town will be blindsided if you sign those papers on their behalf without another town planning meeting. Is that what you want?" Aunt Adeline said.

"Neither myself, nor Holden Investment Partners would continue to financially support the town if you go ahead with this disastrous deal, Mayor Buckalew," Flynn added in a tone of finality.

"Oh, Lord," the mayor moaned.

"I've offered five percent over assessed values for these people's homes. I'll make it ten percent. That will take the sting out of *your* acting in *their* best interests, Mayor," Silas Dale stated.

"An excellent idea, sir," Jonathan said. "With all due respect, though, maybe it would be best to have a town meeting to announce the deal and mend fences. It will be easier if we have the town's cooperation."

Silas Dale shot him a scowl of disdain.

"Just sign the papers, Walter. It's not rocket science," Coralie said. She put them in front of him with a pen.

I felt sick with what I was about to say. "Mayor, there's been an arrest. There won't be any more murders."

Surprised looks went around the table.

The mayor said, "Who? Who did Derek Gordon arrest?"

"Betsy Bell Ward," Aunt Adeline said.

"What? That child couldn't hurt a fly," the mayor blustered.

"Perhaps not flies, but clearly two people," Coralie said and pressed the papers closer to the mayor.

I wondered what she might be getting out of the deal. Money, probably.

"Maybe so," Aunt Adeline said. "The point is that the murders had nothing to do with Jane Austen Town. They were personal. And while I will never condone the loss of life, I must point out that news of the murders has given the town a lot of publicity that couldn't be bought. We'll be updating people as to the dates for the next Jane Austen Festival. We'll be working together as a community to make the next one even better for the attendees and for us financially. To my knowledge, we've not lost a cent putting this festival on. On the contrary, when we add everything up, I'm sure we'll be surprised at the profits. There's no reason to jump off the cliff while we're on the path to success."

The mayor smiled at her.

Coralie looked like she wanted to pick up the sleigh of pretzels and throw it at her.

Jonathan Warren kept a poker face.

Silas Dale shot to his feet. His face was red. "No! There will be no mamby-pamby town meeting. Adeline Starling! You are nothing and a nobody. Just an old woman who likes to dress up like its Halloween all the time. So what if your four times great granddaddy or whoever had a hand in founding this small town? That was then and this is now! Drag yourself out of the past, woman! Mayor Buckalew, Coralie said you would sign those papers. Do it now!" he shouted.

After the ring of his brash words, the silence that followed seemed equally loud.

But I felt some relief from the awful tension. Silas Dale had made a mistake. Silas Dale had insulted Aunt Adeline to her face, in front of people. One didn't behave like that and get away with it in Jane Austen Town.

Aunt Adeline sat with the faintest of smiles on her face.

The change in the mayor was immediate. He sat up straight and assumed an air of authority "We'll discuss this again after the holidays, after we've totaled the money made on festival. That's my final word."

Silas Dale rounded on him. "I do not accept defeat. But you will. I'll make sure you're not re-elected. Coralie, thank you for your hospitality, but I'm leaving. Jonathan, get the car and take me to the airport."

"Yes, sir," Jonathan said. As he left the room with his boss, Jonathan turned and smiled at me.

Later that day, I couldn't help but admire Brock Winthrop's way of dealing with legal matters. He listened to what Flynn and I had to say about Sharon and told us he would handle it discreetly.

Afterward, Flynn claimed he had promised to go with Hugo to the hottest ticket in town, the Open Mic Evening. As wine was being served, it promised to be great fun with music, songs, poetry and photo opportunities. Regency costumes were encouraged. Hugo had asked me for a copy of a bawdy English country song. I'd given him "The Fair Maid of Islington" despite my better judgement. I hoped Neil would be there for photos for the *Jane Austen Town Gazette*.

During a quiet dinner that night at Starling Farm—Aunt Adeline had invited Brock to stay with us overnight—the attorney explained that Detective Gordon had heard from Forensics. The knitting needle that killed Alexandra had a partial print of Betsy Bell's right thumb. That was the evidence he needed to arrest her.

"But Betsy Bell sells knitting needles in her store," I protested. "Naturally her prints would be on them. Maybe the killer bought one from her."

"Could be." Brock nodded

"And what did Betsy Bell say about the disposable gloves Neil told me he saw her buy at Monday's?" I asked.

"She uses them when she cleans her apartment and the store so her hands don't come into contact with cleaning solutions. Betsy Bell said her mama taught her that a lady always keeps her hands nice."

"Well, she's right," Aunt Adeline said.

Brock then told us that when Detective Gordon heard about Sharon, he'd listened and then burst out with "And Sharon knits! She'd have a supply of knitting needles!" and had then thrown his hands in the air and muttered something Brock didn't catch about getting a job in Richmond.

While he couldn't get Betsy Bell out of jail that night, Brock and Aunt Adeline had done everything they could to make her comfortable. They brought her favorite toiletries, a cozy blanket, and a copy of *Northanger Abbey*, Betsy Bell's favorite Jane Austen book. As they were leaving, Percy had come in with a book of William Cowper's poems. Aunt Adeline said Betsy Bell had plenty to keep her mind off of her surroundings or at least make them bearable.

Ida Calhoun wasn't in the house tonight. Brock assured us that Detective Gordon would investigate Sharon quietly as he'd already made an arrest in the case and didn't want to look like a clown. Aunt Adeline and Brock continued to talk and theorize, but I'd zoned out.

Oh Jane, I thought, holding my pendant, it's been right in front of me all along and I couldn't see it. Didn't want to see it, maybe.

In something like a trance, I said goodnight to Brock as Aunt Adeline went to take him upstairs and show him the guest room. She turned and looked a question at me. I managed to smile and nod, reassuring her I was fine.

Alone in the dining room, I stared into the fire, then picked up my phone. I needed to talk to Jonathan to make sure he'd come to the ball tomorrow night. It didn't matter what people thought. I needed him there. I tried his cell phone, but there was no answer. I hoped he hadn't gotten on that plane with Silas Dale. I dialed the Stay a While motel in Charlottesville. But, Merry Lee, the chatty receptionist said she hadn't seen him. He hadn't checked out so I left a message for him.

Cho walked into the room and meowed at me. He sat down at my feet and looked at me. "Well, Cho, I'm not exactly the best amateur sleuth, am I?"

"Meow," he said urgently.

"Remember when Louisa Musgrove from *Persuasion* fell and hit her head? She was unconscious for a while and must have been very confused when she woke up. That's how I feel."

Or maybe it was clarity that I felt. A depressing clarity.

Cho jumped up on the green chair. He rubbed his jaw on his favorite painting.

"I know, I know. Come on, let's go upstairs. I need to call Hayley for help. She's my ride or die."

Chapter Twenty-Two

J ane Austen's 250th birthday dawned gray and considerably
colder. I huddled under my quilt. Last night, Hayley had listened to what I needed and told me she'd get on it. I checked my
phone, but there was no message from her.

I'd had a hard time getting to sleep the night before with theories
and questions running through my mind. Around two, I'd finally
put on the 1995 adaptation of Pride *and Prejudice* and let it run. I
drifted off to Charlotte Lucas telling Lizzie she wasn't romantic.

Since it was after ten, I forced myself to get out of bed and take a
shower. When I came out, bundled in a warm robe, Aunt Adeline
was coming in my door, a tray of food in her hands.

"Aunt Adeline, you didn't have to bring me anything. That
coffee sure smells good though. Hmm, are those sausage biscuits
and gravy?"

"They are."

She sat on the bed while I ate. "We've had to cancel the big garden party and picnic. It's only in the forties outside. We've moved everything to the church hall and are showing the 2009 adaptation of *Emma*. Hayley's been run off her feet between overseeing the picnic food and putting the final touches on the supper food for the ball tonight. Valeria is helping, of course, but it's a lot."

"In the forties? Does that mean we're getting snow tonight after all?"

"That's what the weather people are saying."

"I wish I could help Hayley. With this arm, I'd be useless but I feel guilty she's working so hard."

"How's your arm today?"

"It doesn't feel quite as bad. The swelling's down. Is Brock still here?"

"He left around six this morning. He thinks Derek will be questioning Sharon today."

Feelings I couldn't capture in words threatened to overwhelm me. I couldn't go to Detective Gordon yet. I needed all my facts in order, with proof, first.

"Kay, you're white as a sheet. Maybe you should try to sleep."

"No. It's Jane's birthday. I need to be up and doing things."

Aunt Adeline smiled. "If that's the way you feel, you can come down to the kitchen and help me make Regent's Punch. I've got all the ingredients and thought Hayley could serve it in my Regency Old Sheffield silver punch bowl. Won't that look nice on the supper table at the ball?"

"Yes, it will be much appreciated by all considering the heavy alcohol content. By the way, where's Mrs. Calhoun?"

Aunt Adeline stood. "We agreed she needn't come into town today with the possibility of snow."

The two of us not only made the punch, but also put together my special recipe for candied bacon crackers.

As twilight fell, a light snow began to fall.

Aunt Adeline and I rushed to the window to look out. We didn't get snow very often in our part of Virginia, so it was always an event.

Mr. Woodhouse from Emma would be horrified at the snow.

"I suppose we'll drive to the ball," I said.

"Flynn is taking you, me, and Guthrie in his Lexus."

I bit my tongue. When had this been arranged and why wasn't I informed?

Before I could work myself up, my phone chimed. A text from Hayley!

Crazy here. Twelve waiters to train. Not even in my ballgown yet. No final word on your question. I sent it to a friend who knows about these things. Not looking good. Watch yourself!

***

When the doorbell rang, I picked up the train of my sea-green silk gown and went to answer it. My right arm was in the pretty lace sling Betsy Bell made for me. I pulled the door open with my left, which was covered in a silk white glove that ended above my elbow.

Flynn stood there looking like he'd time traveled from the Regency era. He wore a deep burgundy colored coat over black breeches. A snowy white cravat, tied perfectly, rose from an ivory vest with embroidered gold-colored acorns. White gloves covered his hands.

He bowed. "Good evening, Kay."

I dropped into a curtsey. "Flynn. You look...historically accurate," I told him with a smile.

"I dare not be anything else," he quipped, one eyebrow raised. "You're very lovely in that pretty shade of green."

As I looked into his eyes, I had a sudden urge to unburden myself and tell him everything.

At that moment, Guthrie, looking every bit as handsome as Flynn in a slate-colored coat over black breeches, climbed up the stairs.

I motioned both men inside as Aunt Adeline descended the stairs.

Guthrie swept her a bow. "Addy, my dear, you are regal tonight."

In her purple satin with a tiara made with amethysts, my aunt did look like royalty. She'd taken the food and punch down to the Assembly Rooms earlier, and now took Guthrie's arm as he led her to the car.

When we approached the Assembly Rooms, I gasped. I felt I had entered an Austen adaptation as I gazed upon people in Regency dress (required for the ball) walking in the light snow. Men with torches lit the way.

Flynn parked the car and first put my faux fur cape around my shoulders, then offered me his arm. Aunt Adeline and Guthrie walked ahead. Inside, we could hear the noise of voices coming from upstairs. At the entrance to the building, the room where children took art classes was put to use as a cloakroom. We left our outerwear with my niece, Sarah Beth, who was dressed in white muslin.

"Mom said I could come upstairs and watch the dancing," she told me.

"Are Josie and Bobby here already?" I asked.

"Yes. Uncle Neil, too. He's taking pictures of people in this archway of Christmas greens they made up. I guess it's for people to take selfies."

"Selfies? Not very Regency, is it, Kay?" Flynn teased as he guided me to the stairs. Mr. Fulton from the bank, in Regency dress, accepted peoples' tickets to the ball.

I snuck a look at Flynn. I could almost think I liked him.

Yeah right, Kay. You know he's so hot you'd rather watch him walk in those breeches than eat Aunt Adeline's famous fried chicken.

Speaking of hot, whether it was from the multitude of wax candles in standing candelabras and hanging chandeliers or the crush of people, the first thing I felt when we entered the ballroom was the heat. Too bad I couldn't employ a fan like many of the ladies were doing. Then there was the wonderful smell. The large room was perfumed with abundant floral arrangements, many of them roses, which stood on waist-high pedestals shaped like Roman columns. The wood floors, what I could see of them, gleamed.

Chairs with red seat cushions were arranged along the walls among tall, potted fern trees. Mirrors in gilt frames hung on the walls to reflect light and the dancers. Musicians in the gallery at the long end of room were tuning their instruments. At the opposite end of the room from the musicians above a large fireplace was a wide, royal blue banner with a shining silver silhouette of Austen that read "Happy 250th Birthday, Jane Austen!"

I felt a burn of tears behind my eyes and reached for my Jane pendant.

"Are you all right, Kay? Arm giving you trouble?" Flynn asked.

"No, no I'm fine. It's all so beautiful. I almost feel like Jane herself could walk into the room."

Aunt Adeline appeared at my side. "One cannot have too large a party as Mr. Weston says in *Emma*. Although I think we've come close. Listen, Kay, Hayley is running between the kitchen and that curtained off room over there. That's the supper room. She's setting up food. She told me to tell you 'It's fake' whatever that means."

Reality returned with a sharp sting. I craned my neck and looked around the room. Could Detective Gordon be here? Then I spotted him, the lone person from 2025, dressed in a business suit. I had to talk with him.

"Kay, did you hear me?" Aunt Adeline said. "I'm going to call the first dance, a minuet. Old fashioned for the time period, but even the Prince Regent held a ball which started and ended with one. You know the steps, of course."

"Y-yes, although I shouldn't dance considering I only have one working arm. I'd be worse than the clumsy Mr. Collins in *Pride and Prejudice.*"

"I know the minuet having danced it in Colonial Williamsburg. I'll partner you, Kay," Flynn said.

Aunt Adeline smiled and walked away.

My eyes swung to his. I didn't know if I should dance with him.

At that moment, a disturbance came from whoever was holding a microphone. The crowd quieted. I saw Aunt Adeline take Miss June's arm and walk her over to Francie. The whole time Miss June shouted that she should be the one to give the news. But it was Mimi Monday, dressed in a red gown, that said, "Ladies and Gentleman, Lorraine Longo has, only moments ago mind you, given birth to a healthy little girl she's named Jane!"

Oh, Lorraine, your Jane couldn't wait another day, no less two weeks.

Laughter and applause broke out.

Aunt Adeline waited for it to die down then said, "The minuet!"

She and Guthrie took their places among the dancers.

The musicians struck up Beethoven's Minuet In G, a light playful tune, but as I performed the steps with Flynn, it didn't feel light and playful when his gloved palm met mine. The look on his face was inscrutable.

It felt as if the whole room watched us perform the intricate steps of the dance. Flynn was an excellent dancer, I had to admit when I could take my mind off my steps for a moment.

Around us, everyone looked happy, and while the dance was not performed perfectly, people laughed at their own mistakes.

The dance didn't allow for much conversation and it ended quickly.

Everyone clapped and waiters circulated with glasses of Roman punch, something Flynn waved away.

My phone vibrated in the pocket of my gown.

"Excuse me," I said to Flynn.

I vaguely heard him asking a waiter for something.

It was a text from Hayley. I felt a chill in the hot ballroom as I read the words. The enormity of their meaning washed over me leaving me horrified.

When I looked up, Jonathan Warren was standing in front of me.

"Hello, Kay, I came after all, since you asked. You look beautiful. Is my costume all right? I had to rent it from the UVA theater department," he said, indicating his black coat and breeches.

Where had Flynn gone?

I looked at Jonathan and shivered.

His dimples disappeared and his brown eyes bore into mine. "Are you cold? I hope you're not coming down with something. My daddy used to take a tablespoon of turpentine-like medicine mixed in orange juice if he felt a cold coming on."

"Why?" I asked. "Why did you do it?"

Aunt Adeline announced a Scottish reel and the lively music began.

Jonathan put his arm around me and led me behind a potted fern near the supper room.

Away from others, he looked at me intently. "What are you talking about?"

"You didn't drive from New Jersey to Charlottesville on Friday morning. You were in Charlottesville Wednesday night. Plenty of time to kill Nathaniel Grant on Thursday. You see, I talked with Merry Lee at the Stay a While Inn. You made quite an impression on her. She told me you'd been at the motel since Wednesday night."

He let out a heavy sigh. "She's mistaken. I showed you the security footage of me at the New Jersey casino on Thursday night."

I shook my head. "Fake. The TVs are angled, but, if you look closely, the picture on the TVs is straight up-and-down. It's been superimposed. You must have taken it from Thursday's game and put it over the footage from a different day that you were actually at the casino. I knew something was wrong when I saw the customers at the bar. They weren't watching TV; they were on their phones or talking to one another. If they were betting on the game, why didn't they pay attention to it?"

"Kay, this is crazy talk. You're wrong," he insisted.

"No, I'm not. You killed Nathaniel Grant, and then you killed Alexandra Bartholomew. You went to Betsy Bell's store, Happy Fabrics, and stole a stainless-steel knitting needle. That's why it has a partial print from Betsy Bell on it and the rest is wiped clean. You used gloves so your prints aren't on there. You tried to frame Betsy

Bell for both murders, first by using her scissors, then the knitting needle."

He looked at me like you would a small child who'd been naughty. "Kay, have you been taking strong painkillers for your arm?"

"It's not crazy. It's the truth. Only you had me so fooled. Everyone distrusted you but me. Why did you do it? Why did you frame Betsy Bell? Tell me," I demanded. "Or I'll get Detective Gordon, and you can tell him."

Jonathan's head turned slightly. He darted a glance in the detective's way. When he looked back at me, it was like seeing a different person. Gone was the boyish look and in its place was a mocking sneer. "You should be grateful to that bird that made you fall," he said. "Otherwise, you'd be dead."

Shock held me speechless. Suddenly, his words at the hospital came back to me, the ones I knew didn't ring true but couldn't put my finger on what was wrong.

"I shouted when I saw the person draw back the bow and I realized their intention. But I was too late."

I'd never heard a shout. That was what I had tried and failed to remember.

"You never called a warning. You wanted me dead."

In a flash, he took my lace sling over my head and tossed it behind the potted palm. My injured arm hung down.

"You can't get anything right," he snarled. "I stole two of those knitting needles from that idiotic woman's shop. I'm holding one of them. You either come with me, or I'll slide this into your heart the way I did with Alexandra. She should have known not to go out on dates late at night with handsome strangers. And she should have known not to argue with people in public. Like the fabric store owner."

I knew if I went with him, he'd kill me. He'd already tried to kill me. I took a step away from him when the sharpest pain I'd ever felt in my life zigzagged up my arm. He stood very close to me shielding his actions from everyone. He had his hand around my injured arm, his thumb pressing down on directly on the wound.

"Everything okay over here?" I heard Josie ask.

He covered it with a supposed loving arm around me, but I felt the sharp end of a knitting needle go through my dress and prick my skin.

"Fine," Jonathan said. We were just going to slip in the supper room for a moment alone."

"Okay," Josie said.

I couldn't say anything. What if he hurt her too?

I dared not cry out for help as he'd kill me right here and now and bolt before anyone knew what had happened.

In a few steps, we were behind the curtains and inside the supper room. Candles on the tables lit the room, illuminating the food and floral displays.

"We'll wait here a minute then leave. You are coming with me, Kay."

"No way."

He pressed his thumb against my wound again and the room grayed out. The pain was massive. I was going to pass out.

Then he released his thumb but kept the knitting needle pressed against me.

I panted. "Tell me why you did it. It was the casino, wasn't it? Did Silas Dale give you your orders?"

He snickered. "That old man? No. I told him I'd planned to ruin the festival, and he went along with it. He didn't know I planned murder. Now I've blackmailed him for half the company. I won't stop until I own everything."

"What about your sister, Olivia?"

"Sister? What sister?" His eyes glittered with malice.

"There's no space program charity either, is there?"

"Don't be any more stupid than you have to be. Although, because the people in this town are stupid, I've gotten away with murder. Twice."

"Why did you kill Nathaniel?"

"No particular reason. I simply needed someone dead. Nathaniel Grant had lots of people who wanted to kill him, so my chances of getting caught were non-existent. I didn't know the man. I made it a feminine murder with a feminine pair of scissors. No one would suspect me. After all, I wasn't even in town. They'd suspect the woman who owns the shop."

"Her name is Betsy Bell Ward, and you framed her. What about Alexandra?"

"When the first murder didn't shut the festival down, I fig-ured two murders would. When I saw Betsy and Alexandra fight-ing—don't look surprised. I've been going around the festival the whole time. I'm talented at changing up my look and blending in.

Anyway, I put her on my list of possibilities. Her murder would have the added benefit of making Betsy look even guiltier."

I'd never seen him around the festival. What a fool I'd been.

"I really did come to Dogwood Park to talk to you, Kay, make sure you hadn't realized I was the killer. Then I saw the discarded bow and arrow by the tree and, what can I say? The opportunity presented itself, so I took it. You were asking too many questions. I figured that if you cleared Betsy, there was always Sharon. But like I said, you were in the park, all alone, so I took my shot, so to speak."

I sucked in a breath at the face of evil.

"Someone has to be punished, and it won't be me. Betsy won't be missed."

"She most certainly will be missed! Everyone loves her. And, she's innocent," I protested. "How can you let her take the blame?"

"Kay, I know you don't have the intellect to understand, but try. Money is *everything*. People like the ones in this town who have none are stupid, despicable, and unworthy. Their lives don't mean anything. Now, let's go or I'll kill you right now and leave your body here for everyone to find."

I swayed and brought up my good arm so that I could press my temple with my hand. "I'm going to faint," I muttered weakly.

I let my body go limp.

I started to fall.

He brought his hands up to my shoulders to steady me.

Exactly like I thought he would.

I curled the fingers of my good arm inward. With all my might, I slammed the heel of my palm upward and into his nose, causing him to cry out and fall backwards onto the floor, groaning in pain, nose bleeding profusely.

"You should know, Jonathan, that my courage always rises with every attempt to intimidate me."

Flynn and Josie rushed into the room.

Flynn took in the situation. "Get Detective Gordon, Josie. Quietly, mind you. I won't have Mr. Warren here ruin Jane Austen's birthday ball." He unwound his cravat from around his neck and tied Jonathan's hands behind his back.

"She's broken my nose! I need a doctor," Jonathan gulped.

Standing with his foot on Jonathan's back, Flynn ignored him and looked at me.

"Jonathan's the killer," I said. "He was going to kill me."

"But you stopped him. Kay, you absolute legend. Are you all right? Over there on the table, there's a blue Jane Austen cupcake that might revive you. I know you like those. I'd grab one for you, but I'm a bit busy."

I started laughing.

Detective Gordon burst into the room. Fast as I could, I told him everything.

"And I've got Sharon in a holding cell," the detective said and shook his head.

"I'm sorry," I said.

"You'll need to come in and make a statement, Kay. In the morning will be soon enough."

"I want an attorney and a doctor," Jonathan demanded.

Derek pulled Jonathan up by Flynn's cravat. He narrowed his eyes at him and said, "You are under arrest for the murders of Nathaniel Grant and Alexandra Bartholomew and the attempted murder of Kay Starling. You're walking out of here with me, now. Not one word will come out of your lying mouth. You will not disturb this party. If you do, I'll make sure you can't call anyone. And the only thing you'll have to drink is some Hurdee Gurdee soda that we confiscated from the empty bottling plant last October after it had been out in the sun for a month."

"Too bloody right," Flynn said.

Hayley arrived, lovely in apricot colored silk, in time to hear this speech. She gave Derek a smile and a slight bow of her head. When Derek left with Jonathan, all three of us stood and listened for a couple of minutes. There was no disruption of the ball.

Hayley said, "You know what you need, Kay? A glass of that punch Adeline made. Whew, it's strong stuff. I'll be right back."

"I do believe I split my glove," I said to Flynn, looking at the blood-stained, torn silk.

"I'll take care of that," he said. He slowly rolled the glove down my arm and tugged it off my fingers. His eyes never left mine.

Maybe I was going to faint after all.

"I claim the next dance, Kay. I believe it's the supper dance."

"It's not historically accurate for me to dance without wearing gloves," I told him.

"Sometimes, we have to make exceptions," he said. He picked up my lace sling and secured it on my bad arm.

I heard the strains of Mr. Beveridge's Maggot begin, the music Elizabeth and Darcy danced to in my beloved 1995 adaptation of *Pride and Prejudice*.

I smiled. "Thank you, yes."

As we exited the room, I saw Hayley holding a glass of punch and talking to Hugo. He took the glass from her, drank the contents and then pulled her on to the dance floor. It appeared she was fussing at him the whole time.

Aunt Adeline danced with Guthrie.

Josie and Bobby danced together. Sarah Beth sat on chair next to a smiling Serenity, her eyes glowing at the scene in front of her.

When I began to dance with Flynn, Neil gave us the thumbs up and took our photo.

Later, after the music was over, waiters immediately began circling with glasses of champagne. Led by Valeria, other waiters wheeled out a cart with the huge, six-layer birthday cake Valeria had designed and made. As she promised, each layer featured one of Jane's books, with miniature fondant pieces depicting miniature people and places from each book. It was a work of art. Oohs and ahhs went around the room.

I accepted a glass of champagne and took a rather large sip. Well, more like a gulp.

To my surprise, Flynn accepted a glass. "Cake before supper?" he said.

"We're living dangerously tonight," I told him.

Aunt Adeline got everyone's attention. She was glowing with happiness which gave me a deep satisfaction.

She raised her glass. "To Jane! Happy Heavenly Birthday!"

Everyone held up their glasses and cried out, "To Jane!"

Flynn helped pass plates of birthday cake around.

The crowd grew jovial as the curtains were opened to the supper room.

I stood where I was for a moment. My gaze rested on the silhouette of Jane Austen on the large banner suspended above the fireplace.

"Happy Birthday, Jane," I whispered. "Thank you for all you've given the world. And thank you for saving our town."

Epilogue

Christmas Day

"That boy was so evil he could destroy the world with a paper plate," Hayley mused lazily. She was doing her best to recline in an overstuffed chair, claiming she was still exhausted from all the baking she'd done for Jane Austen's birthday.

We had spent the morning in church. Now everyone was sprawled out in the gold and cream-colored living room at Starling Farm enjoying the fire and the Christmas tree. Christmas carols played in the background. We had to rest in order to get ready to feast around two o'clock. Aunt Adeline had been preparing food for the last three days. Ida Calhoun was home with Sharon and Palmer, who had time off from school for the holidays. I felt bad that I hadn't been of much help cooking. I'd finished my antibiotic, and my arm was better, but I still wore a sling.

"I don't want to think about Jonathan or my lack of judgement," I said, reaching for my hot chocolate. "Derek said he'd never get out of prison."

"I'm relieved the killer wasn't anyone from our town," Serenity said.

"That's the downside of having strangers in town," Hugo said. "You never know what kind of people you'll get."

"We had good people come! Janeites are good people Hugo Starling," Hayley scolded. "I won't let the festival be judged by one psychopath. Besides, everyone had to make money after the bottling plant closed. Having our Jane Austen festival and birthday party was a whole lot better than letting Silas Dale take over."

"I know that," Hugo said, staring out the window. "Just stating facts."

I frowned. Hugo had been restless since the festival ended.

Neil put newspapers on the coffee table. He handed one to me. "Kay, this is a special birthday edition of the *Jane Austen Town Gazette*. There's a photo of you and Flynn on the front page."

"Thank you, Neil." Looking at the photo, my mind went back to the first dance I'd had with Flynn that night. I hadn't heard from him since and reminded myself that he'd never said he planned to stay in town.

Josie looked up from where she and Sarah Beth were putting together a Jane Austen puzzle. Bobby was glued to what sounded like a game on his phone. "Where is Flynn?" Josie asked.

"He's in London visiting family," Hugo replied and went to sit next to Bobby, pulling out his own phone.

Hayley caught my eye. I smiled like absolutely nothing in the world was wrong. It was Christmas. Time to be with family.

Aunt Adeline came up from the kitchen, Cho bounding in front of her, doing the cat I-will-trip-you dance.

"Hey Cho," I said, reaching my hand out to him. He chirped at me, but jumped up on a plush, gold footrest that had been pushed over by the fireplace. He laid down and assumed an air of curiosity about the proceedings.

Aunt Adeline looked at him, twisting the Christmas apron she wore until the festive teddy bears were unrecognizable.

Everyone looked at her expectantly.

"I've been keeping something from y'all regarding Cho," she began. "But I think you should know why I don't want people outside our family and close friends to know what Olive told me about him."

"What did she say? You know you can trust us," I assured her.

Murmurs of agreement went around the room.

"Cho is a special cat," Aunt Adeline said. "He's Siamese royalty. In fact, he's the King of the Siamese Cats. He never dies. Olive has had him since the early seventies and has entrusted me with his care. She said there may be kidnap attempts on him. That's why we have to keep him safe."

Hugo had a coughing fit.

I couldn't look at Hayley.

Cho lounged, impervious to the talk about him. He began washing the kink at the end of his long brown tail.

Serenity said, "I know you're the best person to care for Cho, Adeline. If you need help at any time, you only have to let me know."

Aunt Adeline smiled. "Thank you for understanding, Serenity. I knew you would."

The sound of the back door closing reached us.

"Is that Betsy Bell?" I asked.

"No, Percy took her down to Florida to see her parents for the holidays," Aunt Adeline said.

Guthrie walked into the room with a festively wrapped package under one arm. "I had to run home for this." He handed the present to Aunt Adeline who began unwrapping it.

I watched as the colorful paper fell to the floor. Aunt Adeline let out a gasp. She looked stricken.

"Guthrie, you didn't!"

"Now, Addie, you know that book belongs with you. I never had any intention of selling it on."

"Oh, is it your first edition copy of *Sense and Sensibility*?" I asked, my voice rising in hope. "The one you sold to pay for the workers groceries?"

"It is," Aunt Adeline answered me then looked at Guthrie. "I appreciate the thought, dearest, but I can't accept it. As a single lady it would be inappropriate for me to accept such an expensive gift from a gentleman."

She held the book out to him.

Guthrie looked into her eyes. "That's easily solved. I reckon you'll have to marry me."

Without missing a beat, Aunt Adeline touched his cheek. "I reckon so."

Guthrie couldn't have looked more pleased if someone handed him *Shakespeare's First Folio*.

After a stunned moment, we all cheered.

"I'll get the champagne and some glasses!" Hugo yelled and headed to the kitchen.

Hayley followed him shouting, "Get the 2004 Dom Perignon!"

As we congratulated the happy couple, I couldn't help but spare a thought for Mayor Buckalew who surely would not be happy to hear that Aunt Adeline was engaged.

I thought I heard the front door open and close but wasn't sure until a voice boomed out, "Merry Christmas, everyone!"

"Dad!" I said at the same time as Josie and Neil.

He and my mother were laden down with large red, glittery bags which held presents. My dad was deeply tanned making his blond hair, which he wore past his shoulders, look even blonder. My mother, dark hair like mine halfway down her back, wore her usual jeans, flowing tunic, and layers of beads.

"Gage! Evie!" Aunt Adeline cried as she rushed to hug them each.

Dad dug in one of the red bags and held up a coffee bag. "Peruvian coffee, Adeline. You'll love it. Evie and I are hooked."

Aunt Adeline took the bag and exclaimed, "Huzzah! I'm always ready to try a new coffee blend. Thank you."

Hayley and Hugo returned carrying trays that held flutes of champagne and put them on the coffee table.

My mother offered me her cheek and said, "Kay, what happened to your arm? I hope you were having an exciting adventure at the time."

I kissed her, then forced a smile. "Yes, exciting indeed."

"How long are you staying?" Hugo asked, shaking Dad's hand.

"We were hoping to stay long enough for Christmas dinner," Dad joked.

Laughter went around the room.

My mother hugged Serenity and admired her Christmas caftan which was red with silver bells embroidered at the neckline.

Everyone talked at once as my parents pulled out presents from their trip to Peru. My mother handed Josie and me each soft alpaca wool sweaters. Blue for me, red for Josie. Neil and Hugo were the recipients of colorful, handwoven Chullo hats. Hugo could barely hide his dislike for his hat, but my parents didn't seem to notice.

Their unexpected arrival warmed me. I was determined to enjoy their time with us because I knew it wouldn't be long before they went out on another archeological dig.

But right then, I noticed it was almost one thirty. I needed to feed my outdoor friends before Christmas dinner.

I put my vintage, red velvet coat on over my sweater dress and went outside.

As I approached the brick folly, I heard cawing overhead.

I first filled the bowls with peanuts, then scooped birdseed to put in the feeders.

When I turned around, I saw Tilney coming in for a landing on the side of one of the peanut bowls.

"Well, I suppose I should thank you for saving my life," I told him. "You did swoop down causing me to fall and avoid the arrow deliberately, right?"

Tilney had stuffed three peanuts layered inside his long, black beak. He slanted his head at me. I imagined him saying, "Of course. I need you around to feed me" and then flew away.

I was still chuckling as I went to pick up a gallon of water.

"Here, I'll help you with that."

I whirled around. "Flynn. I thought you were in London."

"I visited family in London, then Northern Virginia," he said. "But I couldn't resist Adeline's invitation to Christmas dinner. Happy Christmas, by the way."

I really wasn't admiring the way he looked in a forest green sweater, tweed jacket, and well-tailored dark blue trousers. "Merry Christmas. I warn you; Aunt Adeline doesn't drop her standards for the holidays. If anything, she outdoes herself. There'll be baked ham with a sweet glaze, roasted turkey, cornbread dressing, greens, candied yams, sweet and mashed potatoes. For dessert, she made a bourbon fruitcake. And every Christmas we have a layer cake shaped like a Christmas tree."

He finished pouring the water into one of the birdbaths. "Sounds like I should have stopped eating yesterday."

"You'll pass on the sugary treats, though."

He put the jug of water down and straightened. There was an expression on his face I could not decipher.

Suddenly, I felt ashamed of myself. Who was I to comment on his eating habits? "I shouldn't have said that. Please excuse me."

His chest rose and fell as he drew in a breath and released it. "My body doesn't process sugar well, Kay. When I was a boy of ten, I was diagnosed with diabetes. Type one. It's well controlled with insulin, diet, and exercise. The diet part involves avoiding sugar, alcohol, and too many carbs. It's not something I normally speak of—"

"Please! You don't have to tell me anything else. I'm mortified as it is. Forgive me."

He smiled. "Detective Gordon knows. That's how I rated the peanut butter crackers the night he took us all in for questioning."

"Oh."

"Kay, I don't tell people, as it's personal, but I chose to tell you. Now stop looking as if I told you I had a terminal illness and days to live. Let's walk to the house."

I turned my steps to match his still feeling embarrassed. "My parents are here."

"Are you happy to see them?"

"Yes. Yes, I am."

"What else have I missed?"

Thinking to keep things light, I said, "Aunt Adeline announced that Cho is the King of the Siamese Cats. He lives forever, and we have to take special care of him."

"Really? How extraordinary. As I recall, Beau Brummell claimed to have a Siamese cat descended from royalty. Of course, Beau liked to tell tall tales."

I'd forgotten Flynn's views, I suppose you could call them, on animals and their powers. Another change of subject then. "After that, Guthrie and Aunt Adeline agreed to get married."

"They're engaged?"

"Yes."

"I'm happy for them. It's wonderful news, but the mayor won't like it."

"No, he won't. Hayley came up with a set of financials from the festival. We made more money than we thought we would."

"Yes, Adeline emailed me the figures. I think there's so much more potential for Jane Austen Town."

"You do? Are you planning to stay and help us figure out when to have another festival?"

He tilted his head. "Of course I'm staying. I have my late uncle's house and vineyard, the community center, and I purchased the bottling plant."

I stopped walking and stared at him. "You bought the Hurdee Gurdee bottling plant? To what end?"

"I have some ideas, but I haven't decided yet. Perhaps we could discuss it over eggnog."

"I'll make sure you get the kind without alcohol."

"Capital!"

He reached into his pocket and pulled out a blue and white wrapped small box and handed it to me. "While I was in England, I popped into the Jane Austen Centre in Bath. They said this was exclusive to them, so I knew you wouldn't have one."

"How nice of you to think of me." Trying not to appear too eager, I painstakingly unwrapped it, noting the silhouette of Jane Austen on the paper. I opened the thin box. Inside was a silver bangle bracelet. Stamped on it were the words, "Jane Austen 250" a space, and then "1775-2025."

I pulled up the sleeve of my coat and put it on, admiring the way the sun glinted on the silver. "It's lovely, thank you. But I didn't get you a Christmas present."

"It's not a Christmas present. I bought it for you as a remembrance of this special year."

"It has been special," I said and grinned. "I won't ever forget it. Well, I'll try to forget the part about the murders."

We were almost to the back door when it swung open. Hayley stood framed in the doorway.

"Hey, Flynn. Kay, y'all better get in here fast. Your aunt and my mother are about to pitch a fit. You're almost late for Christmas dinner! Make haste! Make haste!"

The End

Read on for lots of recipes!

If you enjoyed this book, please consider leaving a review on Amazon.

To receive Rosemary's newsletter, sign up on her website, www.rosemarystevens.com

RECIPES

Hayley's Apple Fritters

    1 1/2 cups all-purpose flour

1/4 cup sugar

2 teaspoons baking powder

1/2 teaspoon salt

1 1/2 teaspoons cinnamon

1/3 cup milk

2 eggs

3 tablespoons applesauce

2 large Granny Smith apples or Honey Crisp apples peeled cored and diced

Vegetable oil for frying

Glaze

2 cups powdered sugar

1/4 cup milk

1/2 teaspoon vanilla extract

Whisk together dry ingredients in a medium bowl. Don't over-mix. Make a well in the center and add 1/3 cup milk, eggs and applesauce. Stir just to combine. Fold in apples.

Heat 1 1/2 inches of oil in heavy skillet or deep fryer to 375 degrees. Drop about 1/4 cup of batter per fritter into hot oil letting it spread out as you drop. Cook each side until golden brown; approximately 2 minutes per side. Don't overcrowd the pan. Use a slotted spoon to remove. Drain on paper towels.

Whisk together 1/4 cup milk, powdered sugar and vanilla. Immerse each fritter into the glaze. Turn over to make sure both sides coated. Place on wire racks to allow glaze to set. Store the cooled cooked fritters wrapped loosely in paper towels in a brown paper bag. Or serve immediately!

Aunt Adeline's Homemade Chicken and Dumplings

4–5-pound stewing chicken, cut up

4 cups water

1 large onion, sliced

1-2 stalks celery, cut into1-inch pieces

1 Tablespoon salt

1 bay leaf

¼ teaspoon black pepper

¼ cup all-purpose flour

½ cup cold water

Bag of frozen mixed vegetables, or if you've canned mixed vegetables, use 1 pound

In Dutch oven combine chicken, water, onion, celery, salt, bay leaf, and black pepper. Cook at a simmer for 2 to 3 hours or until chicken is cooked and tender. Remove chicken from bones and cut chicken into pieces. If desired, skim fat from broth. Mix flour with ½ cup water and stir into broth. Stir constantly until thickened. Add vegetables and chicken meat. Prepare dumplings (recipe below) and drop by rounded tablespoonsful on top of hot chicken stew. Cover tightly ad simmer about 15 minutes or until dumplings are no longer doughy. Makes 4 to 6 servings.

Dumplings

1 ½ cups all-purpose flour

2 teaspoons baking powder

½ teaspoon salt

1 Tablespoon minced parsley

2/3 cup milk

1 egg, slightly beaten

2 Tablespoons oil

In a medium to large size bowl, combine flour, baking powder, salt, and parsley. Add milk, egg, and oil. Mix together only until dry ingredients are moist. Don't overmix. Makes about 10 dumplings.

Ida Calhoun's Coconut Cake

Ida says this recipe has been in her family for three generations

6 eggs

2 cups sugar

½ cup butter

1 cup hot milk

2 ½ cups flour, sifted

1 teaspoon vanilla

3 teaspoons baking powder

½ cup black walnuts, chopped

Preheat oven to 350 degrees. Separate egg yolks from whites. Reserve 4 egg whites for frosting. Beat egg yolks, 2 egg whites, and sugar at medium high speed with an electric mixer until light and fluffy, about 5 minutes. Melt butter in hot milk. If necessary, cover and put in microwave for 10 seconds. Add ½ cup flour to egg and sugar mixture, beating slowly. Add half of the hot milk mixture, 1 cup flour and remaining hot milk. Then add the rest of the flour, vanilla, baking powder and nuts. Pour into three 9-inch greased and floured pans. Bake 20 minutes. Cool before removing from pans.

Icing

1 ½ cups sugar

½ cup water

4 egg whites

½ teaspoon cream of tartar

1 teaspoon vanilla

2 cups fresh coconut, shredded

Boil sugar and water for two minutes. Beat egg whites and cream of tartar until eggs stand up in stiff peaks. Pour boiling sugar syrup into egg whites, beating at highest speed on mixer. Two to four minutes later, when icing becomes stiff enough to spread, add vanilla. Spread between layers, on top and sides of cake. Sprinkle with coconut.

Gator's Tater Tots Macaroni and Cheese

Note: this is the home version. Gator refused to give me the exact recipes he uses at Gator's.

1 (8 ounce) box elbow macaroni

¼ cup butter

¼ cup all-purpose flour

½ teaspoon salt

ground black pepper to taste

2 cups milk

1 cup cottage cheese

2 cups shredded Cheddar cheese

Bag of frozen tater tots

Extra shredded Cheddar cheese

Cook frozen tater tots as directed on package. While they're in the oven, bring a pot of salted water to a boil. Cook elbow macaroni as per directions on box. While it's cooking, melt butter in saucepan over medium heat. Add the flour, salt, and pepper and whisk until smooth, about 4 minutes. Pour milk in slowly while continuing to cook and stir. Be sure to stir so milk won't burn! After about 4-5 minutes, mixture should be smooth and bubbling. Add in the Cheddar cheese and stir until melted, about 2-4 minutes. Add cottage cheese and stir well for another minute. Drain macaroni and add into cheese sauce until thoroughly combined. Pour into a greased casserole dish. Top with cooked tater tots and sprinkle extra shredded cheddar cheese on top. Bake only until cheese is melted. Serve immediately.

Hayley's Regency Banbury Cake

1 package Puff Pastry, thawed

1 cup Raisins

1/4 cup unsalted butter

1/2 cup Mixed Candied Citrus Peels

1/2 teaspoon Cinnamon

1/2 teaspoon Nutmeg

1/2 cup Brown Sugar

1 Tablespoon Rum or ½ teaspoon Rum extract

1 large egg white beaten

3 Tablespoons white sugar

Preheat oven to 450. Melt butter with brown sugar, then add the candied fruit, spices, and rum in a small saucepan. Cool.

Line a baking sheet with parchment paper. Roll out pastry on a floured surface to a thickness of 1/4 inch. Score two lines across and 2 lines down to make 9 squares.

Drop a tablespoon of fruit filling in each square. Wet the edges of each square with water. With your fingers, squeeze the edges together to seal. Turn each pastry over. Shape into ovals.

Dip each pastry into the beaten egg and then dredge in the white sugar. Place on baking sheet and make three diagonal cuts across each pastry. Bake for 10-15 minutes or until golden brown. Let cool before eating.

Aunt Adeline's Famous Crab Cakes

Aunt Adeline's tip: You can prepare these early in the day. Place them on a cookie sheet and seal with plastic. Bake when ready. This way, you can fix another batch, cook them together, and have enough for 12 people.

1-pound backfin or lump crab meat

4 Saltine crackers, crushed

1 tablespoon fresh minced parsley

½ teaspoon Worcestershire sauce

2-3 shakes of Tabasco sauce

1 egg, beaten

1 cup Duke's mayonnaise, divided

½ teaspoon Old Bay Seasoning

½ teaspoon salt

1/8 teaspoon freshly cracked pepper

Paprika

Fresh parsley sprigs

1 lemon, sliced, for garnish

Preheat oven to 350. Gently pick through crab to remove all pieces of shell. Do not break apart lumps of crab. Combine next nine ingredients except for ¼ of the mayo. Mix well. Gently fold in crab. Don't overmix. Form into six cakes. Place on a foil-covered cookie sheet. Spread each crab cake with an equal portion of the reserved mayo. Sprinkle with paprika. Bake for 20 minutes OR until golden brown. Keep an eye on it as you don't want to overbake them. Garnish with parsley and lemon. Serves 4-6.

Kay's Candied Bacon Crackers

32 Club crackers

10-12 strips of bacon cut into 3-inch pieces. You can use regular bacon or turkey bacon.

3 Tablespoons Maple Syrup

Black pepper to taste, optional

Preheat oven to 300 degrees. Line a large, rimmed baking sheet with aluminum foil. Place a wire rack in pan and arrange crackers on it. Put bacon pieces over the crackers lengthwise. Brush 2 of the 3 Tablespoons of maple syrup over the bacon. Place in pre-heated oven and bake until brown and crispy, usually about 40-45 minutes. Remove from oven, brush with remaining tablespoon of maple syrup, and then let cool on the wire rack for 5 minutes. Carefully transfer to a serving platter. Grind a little black pepper over the crackers if desired. Serve.

Ida Calhoun's Christmas Fruit Salad

1 large apple cut into small pieces

1 large pear cut into small pieces

2 large peeled and sliced bananas

3 peeled and sliced kiwis

3 peeled and separated clementines

½ cup pomegranate seeds

Dressing

1 tablespoon honey

3 tablespoons lime juice

1 tablespoon poppy seeds

1 tablespoon chopped fresh mint

In a large bowl, toss fruits lightly until combined. In a small bowl, whisk dressing ingredients. Slowly add dressing to fruits, combining slowly to make sure fruits are covered. Serve and enjoy!

Special Thanks

I could never have written this book without the care of the best neurologist in the world, Dr. Eric Floranda. A gifted and compassionate doctor, Dr. Floranda was able to control the migraines I had found so debilitating for years following a car accident. I'm grateful to him and thank him from the bottom of my heart.

Many thanks to Jerry Lynn Smith, who writes as Lynn Collum, for listening to my crazy ideas and supporting me with my writing for more years than either of us care to say.

I also want to thank author, collector, and historian Candice Hern for allowing me to include her in my Jane Austen festival. Candice really does do a wonderful talk called 'What a Lady Carried in Her Reticule in the Time of Jane Austen' among others. Her website is well worth taking a look at if you're at all interested in the Regency Era in which Jane Austen lived. https://candiceh ern.com/

Finally, although this book is dedicated to my son, Tom, I must also acknowledge everything he does for me. Well, maybe not everything, as that would be another book, but his daily understanding and support have meant the world to me. Not to mention his delicious cooking! Thank you, Wonderful Son, for being you.

Also by Rosemary Stevens

The Agatha Award Winning Beau Brummell Regency Mystery Series

Death on a Silver Tray

The Tainted Snuff Box

The Bloodied Cravat

Murder In the Pleasure Gardens

The Cats of Mayfair Traditional Regency Romances

A Crime of Manners

Miss Pymbroke's Rules

Lord and Master

How the Rogue Stole Christmas

The Murder A Go-Go 1960s Mysteries

It's a Mod, Mod, Mod, Mod, Murder

Twist and Shout Murder

Secret Agent Girl

Written with Ellery Adams
Pasta Mortem

www.ingramcontent.com/pod-product-compliance
Lightning Source LLC
Chambersburg PA
CBHW020312200626
46814CB00006BA/2206